Hands grabbed me ⸻ stumbled off balance I was shaken and ⸻ Dion hissed in my ear, "Drop that basket and follow close."

His hand kept tight hold of my wrist, pulling me behind him. I no longer knew any more than my ears could tell me of what was happening, but he seemed to know where he was making for and that forced him across the current of a crowd running blindly. The shutters were all up on the lower shops. He turned sharply up a narrow stair at the end of a row that led to an upper arcade. A fat merchant coming down blocked the way. We squeezed flat against the wall and I felt his trembling and heard his terrified wheezing as he pushed past. Above there were fewer people. Dion hammered on a pair of closed shutters and shouted a name. They were opened wide enough for us to slip through and then crashed shut behind us.

A TENT FOR THE SUN

Mary Ray

HODDER AND STOUGHTON
LONDON SYDNEY AUCKLAND TORONTO

A C.I.P. Catalogue record for this title is available from the British Library.

ISBN 0-340-53171-1

Printed and bound in Great Britain for Hodder Christian Paperbacks, a division of Hodder and Stoughton Ltd., Mill Road, Dunton Green, Sevenoaks, Kent TN13 2YA (Editorial Office: 47 Bedford Square, London WC1B 3DP) by Clays Ltd., St Ives plc.

CONTENTS

People in the Book

ROMANS

Urbinus Torquartus	A magistrate of Corinth
Secundus	His brother, an officer in the eighth legion
Dion	His younger brother
Domina Nerea	His wife
Pyrrha	His daughter
Domina Olympias	His grandmother
Rufus	A freedman
Corvus	A slave-dealer
Titus Justus	Former ruler of the synagogue in Corinth

GREEKS

Timandra	Daughter of Praxiades, a ship's captain from Samos
Timotheos	From Lystra in Galatia
Apollos	A teacher from Alexandria
Hegiso Rhodippe Marcella	Slaves in the household of Urbinus
Domina Chloe Aemilia	Wife of a former member of the city council
Metella	Her servant
Nicolaus	Dion's friend

A.D. 67: TIMANDRA AND THE
OLIVE TREES

This year we have had a stormy spring, but today the sun is shining steadily as it does at the beginning of the settled weather, and it looks as if the clouds gathered over the southern mountains will drift away across the Gulf of Argos. This morning, as I put the beans to soak for tonight's meal, I thought how long it had been since I had climbed up to the new plantation to see how the young olives have withstood the winter wind and weather. So I left the housework for once and climbed the hill behind the farm. From here Corinth is out of sight to the north-west behind the square shoulder of the mountain, but I can look east down the road to Chenchraea, and that reminded me of Pyrrha. I first came up that road the day she was born.

Now she is nearly thirteen, and soon I expect Urbinus, her father, will send word that she is coming to the farm for the summer. The city, with the Emperor's household in residence, is no place this year for a well-brought-up girl. It is fortunate that Augustus Nero himself is away in Olympia for the moment, celebrating the games for the second time in nine months and at the wrong season. If there was a god there to notice, I would expect him to be displeased.

I think this year Pyrrha may be ready to ask rather different questions about her mother. When I last went to her father's house in the city, a month ago, I thought how much one winter had changed her; she is suddenly no longer a child. I shall not tell her until she asks, but many things happened that summer nearly thirteen years ago in the house of Urbinus Torquartus that she should understand some day.

Most of the young trees that I can see about me were firmly planted, though one, which must have blown over before midwinter, seems to be sending out shoots parallel with the ground and not upwards. The rest are properly spaced out but all different in shape; there is enough wind for their small leaves to shimmer like the great trees near the farm. I suppose the three of us who were young that year in the house of Urbinus were like young trees which have been nearly torn up by a great wind, and must grow as best they can in the soil and space around them.

I have to think hard now to remember the order in which things happened and to realize that at each stage of the way the road was dark ahead. It began, I suppose, on the day Pyrrha was born, although I was occupied in a very different way when the sun first rose that morning above the peeling walls of a slaver's yard at Chenchraea. I was fifteen, a long way from home, and there seemed to be no living person who would help me.

A.D. 54

1 · CHENCHRAEA

After my father had died, just as the midnight cocks were crowing, I slept for several hours. When I woke bright light was coming in through the doorway of the stable, and the flies had settled on my father's sunken face. The smell was as bad as ever. None of the five slaves sleeping in the straw at the other end had washed during the four days we had been there, and there were two donkeys standing in their filth in a stall in the middle. I did not know who would bury my father; the only thought I had in a mind that seemed mercifully numb, was that he should go to his grave clean, though he had died in dirt. I pulled myself up by the end of the stall, aching all over, and picked up the cracked pitcher.

Outside in the courtyard the full glare of the rising sun dazzled me, and it was already hot. A fat man in a sailor's kilt lay across the entrance to the stable, where he had fallen the night before. He was still asleep, his snores bubbling through his beard as if the wine in his belly would come splashing out if he were turned on end. Sweat was already running on his unwashed body under a mat of dark hair.

I edged past his sprawling legs into the main courtyard of the merchant's house. Light from the water across the quay outside was reflected into the irregular space, built round with an assortment of buildings and sheds. The leaves of the straggling vine, which covered the trellis above the doorway to the main room, were already withering, and nothing else grew except in the corner where the spill from the well had made a slimy trail from the midden to the kitchen door.

I steadied myself against the wall and looked across warily at a group of men who were already drinking on benches under the dusty shade. They looked like sailors newly off a boat, still in the salt-caked rags of the last voyage, already swilling down wine in the thorough, cheerless way of men who must get the flagons inside them before they can begin the business of the day. They were a mixed group, two Greeks, a red-haired man who looked as if he came from somewhere to the north, and a dark-skinned Egyptian with long greasy ringlets. I hoped they would go on throwing crusts at the dog until I had fetched my water from the well.

As I reached the kitchen I ducked back into the doorway because the Egyptian was looking my way. The smell from the crusted cooking pots on the hearth made my stomach knot and a bitter taste come into my mouth. I measured the distance again between the well and the restless men. All I was thinking about as I shuffled across the remaining distance with the pitcher in one hand and the torn skirt of my under-tunic hitched up with the other, was why I needed the water. I fixed my eyes on the trailing well-rope and the wet skin bucket.

Bare feet make no sound, but a shadow swooped across the baked mud wall in front of me and I jerked to one side as fingers clawed at my shoulder.

They stood around me in a leering ring, already reeking of wine, beyond the reach of pity even if they could have known what had been happening to me. I glanced back towards the kitchen where a fat slave-woman was standing with her hands up to her mouth, but she would do nothing to help me.

I shouted when the Egyptian reached for me, but it was in anger, not a cry for help. Where would that come from in a harbour where there were fights every hour and girls were either willing or had learnt to take care of themselves? I fumbled at the shoulder of my tunic for the pin that held the folds.

A man laughed. "Come on, darling, strip for us. We'll play while you dance!"

"And afterwards!"

The words were like a blow, and I fell back. Then the ring closed in. As I jumped to one side, throwing out my arm to steady myself, my foot slipped in the patch of mud and the pitcher I was holding crashed back against the wall, shattering so that only the rim and one broken handle were left in my hand. In some strange way this seemed to pierce the numbness and hurt more than anything that had happened in the last few days. I threw the shards in the face of the dirty-mouthed Greek, wrenched my pin loose, and raked it down over the Egyptian's clutching hand. He yelled, pulling it back with a red beaded line springing across the dark skin.

Behind them I saw the sailor come awake with one belch. He made straight for the Egyptian, who was half his size, tossed him out through the gateway with one hand, then looked round him grunting like an angry pig. The last of the men sidled past and out on to the quay as he subsided back into sleep.

I slipped down on my knees, trembling as if I had a fever, my arms wrapped tightly round my body and the torn shoulder of my tunic.

There were voices outside the gateway. A tall man stood there with the light behind him and at the sight of someone unfamiliar I forgot even my broken pitcher; all I wanted now was to hide in the dimness of the stable.

It was still so dark in there that I could hardly see my father's body. I touched his shoulder; it was already stiff, and I knew it would be difficult to make him lie decently.

He had died curled over on his side like a small child, and alone in the night I had not had the sense to straighten him at once. The slaves were all awake by now and they sat watching me. They were a poor lot, two old men and a skinny woman with her children, but I suppose we had looked no better when the merchant had brought us in four nights before, a speechless, paralysed man and a frightened girl.

As I bent to clear the foul straw from underneath my father's body the light from the door was blocked by some-one coming in. I sat back on my heels and looked up. There were two men, Corvus the merchant, small and twisty with a broken nose, and the tall man I had seen in the gateway. That was the first time I saw Urbinus, and I can remember now not so much what his face was like, because I hardly noticed it, but the impression of orderliness and cleanness that there was about him. From the long smooth folds and fine cloth of his toga I could see that he was wealthy, a Roman and a citizen, in his early thirties.

He ran his eye over the group at the other end of the stable and then saw my father. Once your eyes got used to the light it was plain that he was dead. Urbinus's shoulders went back and he stalked stiffly over to the body, looked hard at my father's face and then briefly at me.

He spoke to Corvus. "When did this happen?" Cold and precise, he must have been a soldier once.

"But, noble magistrate, the man was dying when I took him in. He had the care of his own child, and which of us could ask for more when our time comes?"

"I could, much more. Do you know who he was?"

The merchant looked at me. He had never known.

"Praxiades of Samos, captain of the galley *Pegasos*," I said. And it sounded as unreal to me now as it must have done to the listening men.

"Exactly. And you, Corvus, naturally have no idea how a free man came to die among slaves? Your kindness in taking him in was for the sake of his daughter, I imagine; a nicely brought up Greek girl doesn't come on the market every day. What does it matter if she is legally free if she's a long way from home and you can make a quick sale? If my cargo of wool had come in two days earlier I might have been in time, but the story's stale by now and I only heard a part of it and the name Praxiades of Samos today in the harbour master's office."

For the first time he looked at me properly. "So you are the daughter. Come out into the clean air and tell me what happened. What is your name?"

"Timandra."

There was another man waiting outside in the courtyard, short and sturdily built with a large head and a freedman's cap pushed back on it over thick dark hair. He must have heard what was said inside the stable because he looked at me in a way that was probably meant to be compassionate, but his face was disfigured by a scar from the left side of his mouth across his cheek that seemed to make it hard for him to show what he was thinking. Still, it was he who saw me stop as the clear light showed how thin and filthy my under-tunic was, the only garment I had left.

He took off his own short cloak and gave it to me. Corvus had scurried across the courtyard and was bowing by the benches under the vine, with a fresh jug of wine and drinking cups on the table.

Urbinus waved him away. Then he paused and looked at me hard.

"I suppose you've hardly eaten for days? Half a cup of the vinegar Corvus will be offering us would probably do you some good."

I choked over the harsh stuff, but he had been right. I had

to hold the cup in two hands to stop it chattering against my teeth, and while I drank Urbinus began to talk.

"Timandra, I knew your father; he shipped cargo for me many times across to Ephesus and the islands. Only last autumn he was almost the last captain to take a galley out of Chenchraea at the end of the sailing season with bronze lamps and pottery I was sending to Miletus. Careful and honest and not over-fond of talking he was, and what more can a merchant ask? Then this morning I heard the end of a much-told tale of Praxiades ramming a galley off Salamis, and I didn't believe it till I saw the old *Pegasos* beached at the far end of the harbour. It took me an hour to find out where you were; or rather Rufus did, for it wasn't a creditable story and it was easier to come by at back doors than front."

The young freedman Rufus nodded. "They told me the old captain from Samos was sick, but nothing of a daughter with him."

"And why were you with him, Timandra?" asked Urbinus.

I took a deep breath and began my story, telling it in a quiet, flat voice. It made it easier to pretend that it had all happened to someone else.

"My mother died last year, while Father was away. After that I lived with her brother, my uncle. I was the oldest child in our family, there were two boys after me but they both died when they were little. During the winter, Father was ill. He fell over in the courtyard, and when we picked him up he couldn't speak and one of his legs dragged. The speech came back but it took a long time, and he was late fitting out the galley for this spring and his usual mate had shipped with someone else. Father found a Milesian in the end, but the men didn't like him. When we reached Rhodes three of them deserted and we were delayed again finding some more. The Milesian did it in the end, and Father said they would do, and it wasn't till later that we found out they came from Miletus too."

"That would have made me suspicious," said Urbinus. "But you were with your father? Why?"

"Because he wasn't well. My uncle thought I should be there to cook and look after him, or that's what he said. I think he was thinking there would be one girl fewer in the house—he has three daughters but I'm older than they are. I'd been with my father before, short trips across to Ephesus, and once here to Chenchraea. I don't get sick, and I soon learned not to ask Father questions when we were coming into harbour."

"But now you're grown it was dangerous for you, with your father a sick man," said Rufus.

"I suppose so, but it didn't sound like that when Uncle suggested it. After Rhodes Father was worse, sometimes silent for hours and then going into great rages; and little things started to go wrong again. There was food spoiled and cargo missing. We went across to Paros for a load of marble to bring here, and then the wind turned against us and the last two days were rough sailing and Father wouldn't rest. I don't suppose it would have helped much if he had. Six days ago we were past Salamis and due in harbour by the evening; I was in the little room under the decking at the bows, where we cooked and slept, so I never saw what happened. There was shouting and a grinding crashing noise that went on for a long time, and then the planks above the bunk opposite me splintered and caved in as I watched and the galley settled over on its side."

"So it was the *Pegasos* that was rammed!"

"I don't know, but what they said—the Milesian and the captain of the other boat—was that we hit them. They towed us into harbour, which took a long time as we were riding over on one side because the marble had shifted. Then they beached us away from the main harbour and Father told me to keep the cabin door shut while he went ashore to decide things. That was the last time he spoke to me."

Then I was not simply telling the story, I was back in the hot, disordered cabin with the men outside and my carefully arranged oil and spice jars broken on the floor. I remembered my father's grey face and the jerky way he moved and his look of appalling weariness. Tears began to run down my face and I did not bother to wipe them away.

"I couldn't get the beam across the door so I pushed a chest against it. In the evening the Milesian shouted to me to come out. I didn't answer at first, but then he said Father was ill and he needed me, so I put some things into a basket, a clean tunic and the valuable things I couldn't leave. He took me to an inn close to the water; it was getting crowded as the light went and I remember the first lamps shining across the harbour as we went in. They took me quickly to an inner room, and my father was lying on the floor in the dirt and dog scraps, with his eyes shut and dribble coming out of the side of his mouth."

"How did you get from there to Corvus's yard?" asked Urbinus.

"That was the next day. I sat on the floor all night with my father because no one would help me to lift him, and I wrapped what clothes I had round him because he felt so cold. Sometimes I thought he'd woken up because his eyes opened and he seemed to know me, but he couldn't speak. It took what jewellery I had to buy a blanket and a little food. Then the next evening Corvus came in; I didn't understand who he was at first. He explained that our ship had been so badly damaged that it would have to be sold to pay for what we had done to the other galley. Then he said we would be more comfortable at his house because he would give us food while I nursed my father. I didn't understand, you see, that he was a slave-dealer, and I couldn't have done anything if I had, because I couldn't leave Father."

"It's an ugly story, but clear enough," said Urbinus, getting up. "All hatched before Rhodes, I expect. I must speak to Corvus. Go back to your father now and I'll see they send someone to help you."

The fat woman came with a bowl of water, and linen to wrap my father in. We had finished by the time Urbinus came back into the stable. He stood looking at me with pity and something like a weary acceptance of how things were in his face.

"I've arranged things as well as I can. Rufus has business with a wool merchant that will take him till noon, and then he'll come back for you—and——" he gestured towards the shrouded body. "Now, Timandra, are you listening to me?"

I stood up wearily and looked at him, and I knew before he spoke what he was going to say and that it would not be easy for him either.

"Corvus says he gave money for you and that he thought he was buying you honestly from the other captain. The galley has left already and there's no way to prove the story you told me, although I believe you. He's frightened because he knows I could make trouble for him, and his mind can't be easy, because he's made a very low price for you. But as I've bought you I can't under the law free you again at once, not without legal proofs that might be hard to get. I must tell you, I am not only a merchant but one of the city magistrates of Corinth, this year. But that gives me few special powers. Just because I honour justice I understand how difficult it can sometimes be to obtain it. Now, your uncle, would he help you?"

I remembered my uncle's narrow face, and his look of relief as I had walked down to the harbour of Samos for the last time with my father. That hurt badly enough to make me cry again, so that I could not answer Urbinus but only shook my head.

"From your story that was what I thought. Better to realize it at once than to wait for the answer to a letter that may never come. For the memory of your father I would have taken you anyway, till I could place you in a good household, but it happens that at the moment I need another girl in the house. Rufus will tell you."

He patted me on the shoulder in what was meant to be a reassuring way, and went back into the sunlight.

That was how I came to drive in a wagon up the road to Corinth, late in the afternoon of the same day, in a clean tunic and veil that Rufus had brought with him when he came back for me. The body of my father lay beside our load of woven wool, and Rufus was quiet until after we had turned into the farm, this farm. Phlegon was the overseer then and his people were kind as they carried my father's body away to lie in a quiet room before it could be laid to rest among the old trees. I wondered at first if I would be left there, but clearly Rufus had other orders, and in a way I was glad. The father I remembered had been dead to me ever since I first saw him lying speechless on the inn floor. Now there was no time to mourn him, for I must think for myself, no one else would.

Rufus drove the mules faster as we turned back on to the main road. Most of the farms were already behind us, and there were tall cypress trees on either side of the road, throwing long shadows across the tombs of the wealthy families that were built here outside the walls of Corinth; the city itself was still hidden by the shoulder of a square mountain. The sun had already gone and there were walls like dark teeth along the highest crest against the yellow light in the sky.

Rufus began to talk in a comfortable way that did not seem to need answering.

"Urbinus will be a good master. What else could he have done except buy you? He couldn't have left you alone in Chenchraea, free or slave. I was born on the farm, and he freed me five years ago when his father died, I never thought of anything except to go on in the service of the family. The Torquartii have been here three generations and they're still more Roman than Greek. Their ancestor was a centurion who was settled here when the city was refounded more than a hundred years ago; that's why they have a military name, he won a gold collar serving with Caesar in Gaul. Now the old master's dead there are the three brothers, and Urbinus is head of the family, though his grandmother, Domina Olympias, is still alive—and may the gods preserve her long to bless us."

"Is there a large household?" I asked, suddenly understanding for the first time that tonight I would sleep among strangers.

"No, not really. The family have never been wealthy, although the master has his land. He has needed the profits of his business to support himself in politics—the election to the magistracy cost a lot. Luckily here in Corinth no Roman is too proud to engage in trade, they'd starve if they were among all the Greeks! You know, Timandra, you're coming to the house on a strange day. Our young mistress, Domina Nerea, went into an early first labour last night and the master is afraid for her. A month ago her own maid, who had been with her since she was a baby, died of a fever. That's why you will be coming at a good time, if she takes to you."

"You said there were three brothers."

"Yes, but Secundus is mostly away with his legion in Dacia, though he's on leave at the moment, and young Dion is only a boy."

"That's a Greek name!"

"Yes." Rufus laughed but in a kindly way as if he was fond of the boy. "I think his father named him Tertius, but no one's remembered that for a long while. He was the last born, fifteen years younger than the master, and his mother was feeling Greek and poetical at the time. Besides, Dion suits him, you'll see. I suppose we're an old-fashioned household really; the house isn't large and not much has changed there since Domina Olympias's day."

There was more traffic on the road now and he had to stop talking. Where it forked he drove off towards the north in the gathering dusk, with the city wall to our left, to go round to the northern gate, for the Villa of the Torquartii lay in that direction, and the way through the market would still be choked with other carts. We turned through the north gates just as the lamps were lit, and up the steep, well-paved road. Almost at once we turned again up a narrow street leading west, and down an alley under a garden wall.

The porter must have been expecting us, because the side gate was opened before Rufus had time to knock.

"What news?" he asked.

"I think the child's born—just."

Rufus drove through the gateway and helped me down. Leaving the cart he hurried me through a narrow yard into an oblong courtyard planted with fruit trees, and with a pillared walk around it lit by the open doors of rooms on the far side.

There was the sound of voices at the far end, and good-humoured, masculine laughter. A girl came out of one of the doorways with a basket of soiled linen in her arms; then I pulled back into the shadows as a tall young man and a boy passed us and paused in the same doorway.

"May we come in now, Urbinus?" the young man asked.

Rufus took my arm to lead me after them, but I drew back again.

"I can't, I'm not clean, after the death last night. I might bring harm to the child."

"That's Greek talk, it wouldn't worry Urbinus. We'll only look."

We had reached the doorway of the room where the child had so recently been born. To one side on a stool beside a wooden cradle an old woman sat with it in her arms, newly washed and wrapped in clean old linen. One fragile, lilac-shadowed hand lay among the folds, spreading like the fronds of a sea anemone. Urbinus, bending over the bed in the corner, hid the woman who lay there. The signs of birth had been cleared away but the room still held the heat of hours of toil and a smell of sweat and herbs.

The baby began to make small noises, snorting like a puppy, and the mother sighed. Urbinus bent closer to stroke her brown hair, that lay still damp over the pillow. I knew then that the child was a girl.

"Let me see her, Hegiso," said the young soldier who must be Secundus, to the old woman.

"Oh no, it's not right," she said, whisking the child away from his outstretched hand. "It's the father who takes her first, if he wills."

She bent and laid the little bundle on the floor. Urbinus was across to it in two paces with a little snort of annoyance, for we had all heard the girl on the bed sob. As he slid his fingers under the tiny dark head to raise the baby the folded linen fell aside and I saw Pyrrha clearly for the first time.

She was large, and the little body between her waving hands was firm and pink. As he took her in his arms, holding her steady in the crook of his elbow, the baby looked up into his face, and the small fingers seemed to reach towards him. I saw his look change from seriousness to amused surprise. With one finger he stroked the soft fuzz of hair and turned towards the bed.

"I must take her to my grandmother."

It was when he moved away that the boy who had been standing back against the wall went over to the bed, and so I saw Nerea and Dion for the first time at the same moment. He was a brown-haired boy, very intent, bending over the dark girl who lay flat and still in her carved bed. Out of the long hours of her labour she had made a life, and even now, when her child was hardly more to her yet than a cry and a dark head glimpsed in her nurse's arms, perhaps the pain seemed worthwhile, because of what it had made.

What had my pain of the last days made for me? Slavery and a drawing in of hope. I think it was then, even on the first day, that I learnt that what would no longer come to me in an ordered way as the daughter of a respectable family in my city, I must learn to grow towards for myself. So an olive seedling must twine its roots between the stones and hold fast till the sun and rain have drawn it up to full growth.

Nerea's pain had had a reason and it had made something. There must be some reason for mine, some power behind the storm that had swept across my life, something that I, too, could still make.

2 · CORINTH

On the day before the *Pegasos* had sailed from Samos my
father had offered a black lamb to Poseidon at the temple
down by the harbour, but I had bought a goose with one of
the last silver coins that had come to me when my mother
died, and I had taken it to the shrine of Isis. I should have
known even then that the voyage would be unlucky, or so I
often thought during those first days in the house of Urbinus,
when it was easier to blame my father than to mourn for
him; a sudden storm had come up over the mountain to the
west, as I was hurrying home from the shrine, and everyone
knew that was always a bad omen.

However, fortune seemed to be shining on Nerea's baby,
she was named Pyrrha on the eighth day, with all the usual
offerings, at the family shrine. There were some in the
household who were not so happy. It was more than a month
before our mistress began to regain her strength and to take
an interest in what was going on beyond the perfumed
security of her own room. By then I felt that I had spent a
year in the house, and not a happy one.

The trouble was that we were divided between the old and
the young. There was the grandmother Olympias, who had
not left her bed for ten years, and old Hegiso, housekeeper in
the days of Urbinus's mother, who was failing now, forgetful
and difficult. Then there was Nerea, and as I came to know

my young mistress better, I could see that she had too gentle a spirit and had been married too early ever to have taken proper control of her household. Things had probably been easier when her maid Prisca had been alive, but without her Nerea was lost, and in no state to instruct me in my duties.

At home in Samos we had been a small family and our two old slaves were part of it; I had never imagined how complicated life could be in a larger household where the slaves were divided into those who attended on the family, and those who cooked and cleaned. As soon as I had been purified after my father's death I should have been attending Nerea, but apart from carrying trays Hegiso would not let me near her; she spent her time sitting and crooning over the baby rather than supervising the kitchen staff. It was surprising that the men of the house got any proper meals after Secundus, who was her favourite, was recalled to his legion. There were times when I went hungry myself, before I learnt that as I was a personal attendant the kitchen people expected me to make do with what I brought back from my mistress's meals, and indeed envied me my first chance at what was left over. Although there always seemed to be enough food being cooked to satisfy the whole household, there seldom seemed anything very much left in the large cooking pots by the time I was able to eat.

It was much the same with sleeping. Hegiso had a mattress on the floor of Nerea's room, the kitchen women each had their own corners in the back parts of the house, and I found that the best place for me was on one of the couches in the summer dining-room, after Rufus had been round to close the shutters for the night. I was usually three-quarters asleep by then, but it was somewhere clean and quiet—the ugly red blotches left by the fleas of Chenchraea had taken a long time to fade.

During the day, when the confusion in the house became

more than I could cope with, I took refuge with Domina Olympias, for her room was often the only peaceful place there was. It was in the southern corner of the garden courtyard, and on the day when Nerea was well enough for the first time to get up in the morning, I remember that I spent long hours there. I had to find something to do each day, because I had never, even as a child, been able to sit quiet with my hands in my lap. During the hottest time after noon I had left Olympias to sleep in peace and had hidden myself at the far end of the house on the terrace that faced north over the Gulf of Corinth outside the summer dining-room. I had no business to be there, but it was cool and deserted and I could see across the city walls not far away to the busy road to Laechium, Corinth's northern harbour.

When I slipped back into Olympias's room the patch of afternoon sunlight had reached across the floor as far as the foot of the bed, but the old woman still lay back against her high pillows with her eyes closed. I thought, as I stood blinking in the doorway, that she was the oldest person I had ever seen; it was impossible to imagine how she had looked as a young bride sixty years before, or even as the mother of a growing son, before the years had twisted her into a small wizened bird-shape with useless hands. A scarf was knotted round her almost bald head, but as usual it had twisted round sideways and her few tufts of hair were sticking up in a white crest. She had the mouth of a shrunken baby, but when she was awake her eyes—screwed deep into the sockets beneath her brows—were wise with all the years of her age.

They opened as I moved out of the doorway and the light flooded back towards her.

"Are you comfortable, Grandmother?" I asked. "Shall I get you something to drink?" Then I put my hand to my mouth. "Oh, my lady, I'm sorry . . . I didn't mean to call you that!"

The old woman eased herself up on elbows that were so sharp they seemed to cut the mattress.

"Why not? Everyone in the household calls me that except in this room, I'm not deaf and I hear them. Besides, I expect you called all the old ladies in your part of the town 'grandmother' and a good thing too; accuracy can be less important than kind intentions. Now, what I really want is a fig. I've been looking at those in the bowl over there and thinking that the longer I waited the sweeter they would taste."

I smiled as I sat down on a stool beside her to cut one into the small pieces that she could manage in her twisted clump of fingers; I should have known Olympias too well by now to think that my mistake would bother her.

"I thought you were asleep," I said. "You should have called me."

"Then the afternoon would have gone more slowly, and I would have had nothing to look forward to!"

While she ate I sat looking out into the golden light of the courtyard, which was broken into sharp patterns of dark and brightness by the leaves of the fruit trees. The figs were ripe and sweet and I started to cut up a second, lost in my thoughts.

"What was it made you cross?" asked the soft, dry voice.

I looked up quickly. Olympias's sunken eyes were sharp and wise.

"Give me that fig before you cut yourself with the knife," she said. "Timandra, I'm learning to know your silences. There are times when you are quiet and heavy and others when you are as tense as an overstrung lyre. What has happened now?"

"Something that makes me ashamed when I'm with you," I said, looking down at my fingers, which were now plaiting the fringed ends of her bedcover.

"I don't think," said the old woman slowly, with the voice of someone who is remembering a great many things as she speaks, "I am being vain when I say that there is not likely to be anything troubling you that I have not felt myself, or seen in someone else before. And it can be helpful to have company."

"I suppose it's hard to tell you just because you will understand so well! I feel as if the walls of this house are closing in around me, Grandmother, even if it is the largest one where I have ever lived. My mother was strict and I wasn't allowed to run about alone at home, but there was the harbour and I did sail with my father sometimes, and I've never been shut in for so long before. Besides, I like to do what I have to do well, but I don't know here what my duties are or where to find things."

"And what makes it so bad this afternoon, apart from Hegiso?"

"Nothing. Well, something so small. Dion was waiting in the atrium for his friend, and when he came they talked for a while and then went off together. It happens every day, but as I watched them go out of the door I think I suddenly understood for the first time what being a slave means. For the first few days I was almost glad that I was being fed and there was a safe wall around me. This afternoon I understood that I would never again go out of a door like that—free and cheerful, with something exciting to do that I'd chosen myself."

And it wasn't that I was jealous of Dion either, I thought, he wasn't someone one could dislike, though there were times when he was funnier than he realized. Perhaps I had envied him, and yet how would life treat a boy who was not only good looking, but had a simplicity that would be no defence against intentional maliciousness that he would not understand? He was sixteen, a year older than I was, with the build and closely waving hair of one of the grave young statues in the precinct of a temple of Apollo. In a month the Isthmean games would be celebrated in honour of Poseidon in the stadium on the level ground above Chenchraea, and he had a chance of running for Corinth in the boys' race. I thought that Dion was probably also seeing himself as the kind of dedicated young victor who might have been used long ago by a sculptor who dreamed of offering perfection to a god. However, I already knew that in the Corinth where we now lived, such an idea was unusual—and unlikely to be successful.

"Were they going to the gymnasium?" asked the old woman, breaking into my thoughts.

"Yes, it will be very hot today."

"When I was a young mother," she said reflectively, "and my child toddled towards the charcoal brazier, I could either snatch him away or let him burn himself, just a little. The pain might save him from a greater pain later. Now with my grandchildren the choice is not so easy. Dion is going to be hurt, Timandra, and I think that I hope it will be small and soon, but there is not very much I can do about it."

"You mean he won't be chosen for the games?"

"Yes. He will be heartbroken of course, and his summer will seem to have been ruined, but really the boy is more a scholar than an athlete, though he doesn't understand himself well enough to know this yet. By winter he will be absorbed by his new school of rhetoric. But if he should win, even if he only goes as far as the Isthmea, I think I should be very frightened. The gathering of athletes there ceased to be an honouring of the old gods long ago; now it is rather more a market for the appreciators and exploiters of the beautiful. His mother was wrong to call him Dion; it's been no help to a boy of his temperament, with a Roman father, to think of himself as a romantic Greek." She finished crisply with a hint of irritation at her long-dead daughter-in-law in her voice.

"I suppose if I had been beautiful instead of dark-skinned and thin I wouldn't have been sitting quietly here with you," I said.

"No, you would not. You would have been one of the newest and most terrified of the girls known as priestesses of Aphrodite, at the grove behind the temple in the city! I was thin, too, at your age, but I filled out after I was married."

"Then I shall stay thin," I said, getting up quickly so that she should not see my face.

"Timandra, be careful. It's easy to hurt a slave—don't begin to think like that, what you must or what you will never do! If something happens that can't be altered, the pain will be worse than it need be."

I shivered in the afternoon heat. Since those days in the house of Corvus the thought of a man, any man, as close to me as a husband would be, was something my mind fled away from as the burnt child that Olympias had pictured would draw back from a fire.

Nerea's voice sounded from the other side of the courtyard. She must be bringing the baby for Olympias to see.

"I can't free you, or turn you into a boy—which you might not enjoy as much as you think—but I can do something to improve the comfort of all of us in the house," said Olympias. "Even if one lives too long to be useful one can still have some influence, like an ugly thing in the corner of a shrine that is honoured because it has been there longer than anyone can remember. Now, tidy me up, child."

I straightened the bedcover and was just combing back her wisps of white hair when my mistress came into the room carrying the baby, followed by Hegiso. Olympias flashed me a look more piercing than I would have thought she was capable of, to warn me to be unobtrusive.

31

Nerea was looking well today, the colour had begun to come back to her cheeks and her face was fuller, so that she did not look quite so strange as she had since Pyrrha was born—a child with a woman's body. Her thick hair was caught back in a simple knot, for she had not yet started to dine again with her husband and she was only dressed for the woman's part of the house, with her thin summer overdress clinging damply in the heat to her full breasts. The baby's dark head nestled against her shoulder; Pyrrha was drowsy and well fed but not yet swaddled. Hegiso fussed in behind them, clumsy on her heavy legs, with a short neck and her thin hair scraped back from the coarse red skin of her face.

"Give her to me," said Olympias. "She looks too full to wriggle far." Nerea settled the baby into the crook of her thin arm.

Hegiso ordered me out of the room with a jerk of her head, but I pretended that I had not seen her.

"Nerea, my child, you look stronger and the little one is peaceful," said Olympias. "It's time we made plans."

"Of course, Grandmother, but what about?" Nerea's gentle face was puzzled.

"Since your poor Prisca died this house has been like a kicked-over beehive, with you in no state to improve things. Now there is a baby to be looked after as well, we must make some changes. Hegiso has worked for the family for many years and I am sure Urbinus would want her life made easier rather than that we should add to her responsibilities. Now that you, Nerea, are well enough to take control again, the supervision of the kitchen and the house slaves according to your wishes is all that should be asked of her. Timandra is young but sensible, and ready to take over Prisca's work and be woken up at nights by the baby. With the help of Rhodippe who treats me as if I was her baby, she should be able to look after us very nicely and also do what marketing we need in the city—the things Rufus doesn't see to. Really, I don't trust his eye over matching thread or choosing spices. Now is that not a good plan?"

She smiled across at the two women with a look as open and guileless as the baby sleeping beside her.

I thought Nerea was relieved that it had been said by someone else, and Hegiso was speechless with surprise; she sniffed hard and seemed about to leave the room without saying anything when Nerea stood up.

"Yes, I think that will all be very convenient. Hegiso, tomorrow you can come to me in the morning as you used to do. I think I must go round the storerooms myself to see how things are after all this time. This is a year when we must avoid any unnecessary waste. Now, will you go and see what's happening in the kitchen? Something smells very strange!"

When the woman had waddled away Nerea sat down suddenly. "Oh dear, was that all right, Grandmother?"

"Yes," said the old woman with a chuckle, "I think that did very nicely. Now, Timandra, take this fat child away, my arm has gone to sleep "

I picked up the warm baby. Pyrrha dribbled comfortably through the shoulder of my tunic, but hardly stirred as I settled her into her cradle in Nerea's room It was the first time I had been alone with her, but I had always loved to help with the neighbours' babies, and something about this child had taken hold of a part of my heart even the first time that I saw her so soon after she was born.

I was tidying Nerea's bed when she came back, looking weary again now, with the sudden weakness of the recently ill. She stood looking at the sleeping child, rubbing her back.

"Does it ache, can I help you?" I asked shyly.

"I don't know; have you got healing hands? I wanted to

be dressed and tidy before my husband came back, but now I'm tired again."

She sat down on the edge of her bed and I helped her to take off her overdress and to loosen her hair. She slid down on to the smooth sheet, her face hidden in her arms, and I began to soothe and massage the muscles of her neck and shoulders in a way that my mother had taught me.

After a few minutes she wriggled and said, "Oh, that feels good. Now farther down."

I looked up from my work to see the angle of the sunlight in through the door. "When will the master come home?" I asked.

"Not till the ninth hour," she said, through her heavy hair.

"There's still time for you to have a rest, and then I can do your hair in a new way to surprise him. Will you dine with the men?"

"No, I don't think so," she said sleepily. "But I could go in and sit with them afterwards. Tomorrow we must be busy."

I pulled the cover up over her and went on quietly tidying the room. I had not been free before to open chests and see what Nerea had worn before she had been ill.

It seemed that the dead Prisca had been a careful servant, for everything was in good order, the undertunics folded and neat, and the long dresses of coloured linen or silk arranged with little bags of perfumed bark among the folds. I found a dress of thin rose-coloured linen with an embroidered border of tiny flowers; it was not the richest dress but one of the prettiest and I was sure it was one of Nerea's favourites. In her jewel box there was a curved silver diadem and matching ear-rings with hanging flowers like the ones on the dress.

I heard Dion come in, fresh from the baths near the gymnasium; then I went to the kitchen to fetch water for Nerea to wash. Hegiso was just coming out with a pile of dishes for the dining-room. She gave me a sour look but did not say anything.

When I came back Nerea was sitting up, looking with interest at the clothes that I had laid ready. We smiled at each other rather shyly; she could not have been more than a few months older than I was, and we were suddenly conspirators in a plot to surprise Urbinus.

My hands felt rough and clumsy as I combed her hair. I had been doing heavy work for the last month, and before that I had not cared for my skin in the way a girl will if there are other women close for her to compare herself with. Still, Nerea had lovely hair to arrange, with a wave in it that helped the gold pins to stay where I put them. I knew how I wanted her to look, and she seemed happy to sit rubbing almond oil into her small hands while I pleased myself.

There was a goddess kneeling to bathe by a fountain engraved on the silver cover of Nerea's mirror. Her hair was piled up behind a diadem in a way that looked old-fashioned if one compared it with the intricate mounds of curls that we were told fine ladies wore in Rome. But Nerea was half-Greek and lived in a province, and there was something old-fashioned about her shy gentleness.

"Don't look yet," I said, as she picked up the mirror. "I haven't quite finished. If you like it I shall be quicker another time."

Urbinus's voice giving an order to Rufus sounded from the atrium.

"Drop the curtain over the door, he'll think I'm resting," said Nerea with a giggle.

When I had finished she studied herself in silence for so long that I thought she was not pleased. Then she shut the mirror into its case and looked up with a smile and a little air of formality, as if she had just remembered that after all we were not two small girls playing at dressing up. "Thank you,

Timandra, that will do very well. Now bring me something to eat here in my room and then go and tidy yourself so that you can attend me later."

I looked down at my overtunic, which had been washed no-colour-in-particular and was dirty from housework.

"I see, we must think about that, too, tomorrow." She undid two keys from her belt. "Look in the second chest on the left in the far storeroom for something to wear tonight. Prisca was about your height."

Urbinus and Dion were dining alone and only one couch was pulled out in the summer dining-room. The evening wind was rising and Rufus had partly closed the shutters on one side and lit the lamps, slim bronze athletes on tall stands, holding bowls above their heads. Yet there was still a warm glow of light coming in to turn Dion's bent head to gold as he leant forward to arrange a pattern of nutshells on the table in front of him. Urbinus, sitting over his wine, looked more like his father than his brother.

He sat upright in surprise as Nerea led the way into the dining-room with considerable dignity.

"Rufus, bring cushions for Domina Nerea," he said, moving over to make room for her beside him.

I arranged them and then stood back as she settled herself beside her husband, looking flushed and pretty.

"Your daughter was well and so was I, so I thought I would surprise you," she said.

Urbinus looked at her with affection. I had seen little of him during the last month, for the clients who came to escort him to the council house or the market arrived each day at dawn and he seldom came home again until the ninth hour even when he was not dining away from home. It was the first time that I had seen him so relaxed and easy; it was a new side to the city councillor and man of business who had bought me in Chenchraea.

"I wish all surprises were so pleasant. Will you drink wine with us?"

Nerea's look of warning told me that it must be a weaker mixture than usual or it would upset the baby, so I hissed at Rufus who was filling a small silver cup from the wine mixer. He grinned and added more water.

I was shy now. I had never waited at a dinner party before, and I was glad that the family were alone. Later I must ask Rufus to instruct me, he would do it better than Nerea, who would be likely to know something was wrong only after it had happened. I presented the cup to her with a little curtsy, and that seemed to be right, because she smiled and motioned me to stand behind the couch.

Dion was staring at his sister-in-law. "Who do you look like?" he asked in a puzzled voice.

"Is it the goddess on the mirror that used to belong to your mother?" she asked.

He nodded, satisfied. They began to talk of nothing very much, as any family does. The Emperor had been ill again and there had been a sacrifice at the temple of Augustus.

"The Suplicii provided the bull and I would take an oath that it was lame, or if it wasn't it stumbled as they were leading it up and that would be an even worse omen. May the gods avert it! Then, my dear, old Aemilius—his eyesight gets worse every month—got too near when the knife man was cutting the beast's throat, and as he was clumsy there was blood everywhere. The poor old man's wife must spend a fortune at the fullers, for his toga was badly splashed. I thought for a moment someone had tried to kill him! Dion, why are you looking as though you've swallowed an olive stone, unless of course, you have?"

Through the laughter that followed I noticed that Dion looked puzzled and a little hurt; however, he smiled and pointed to the table. "There aren't any olives tonight!" Then he was serious again.

"I was wishing I could understand you better, Urbinus. I see the things you do and they make sense, you're very successful and people respect you, but I don't know why you do them. I don't know how you can go to a sacrifice and then laugh at it afterwards. Either the gods are real and killing a bull in their honour means more than fresh meat for the Suplicii, or they're not, and I don't know why you bother to go."

Nerea looked quickly across at her husband to see if Dion had annoyed him, but the magistrate was still smiling benevolently at his brother.

"There are times when I wonder if you walk through life blindfolded like a donkey at a threshing mill! There is much more to be learnt than you will find at the school of Simonides. If the worship of the gods has lasted so long there must be a reason for it, even if it isn't the obvious one. The worship of Poseidon of the Sanctuary or the Emperor is something that unites the citizens and that's important. Besides, who knows, can we afford to leave one thing undone that could bring us good fortune?"

Dion looked across at his brother and then down again at his nutshells. He did not say anything more; this seemed to be an argument that had happened before and I thought he was already regretting that he had started it again.

Urbinus changed the subject. "Was the gymnasiarch pleased with you today?" Dion grinned; they were back on safe ground again.

"I think so. I didn't win but I was starting better. Of course on a good day Nicolaus can leave me standing—and the worst is he doesn't mind if he runs or not!"

"And was it one of the languid Nicolaus's good days?" inquired Urbinus with a look that made me sure he disliked the boy.

"Yes it was, he was cross about something and that makes him go like a deer."

"He's nearly a year older than you are!" said Nerea.

"And old for his age! Surely you didn't run all afternoon in this heat?" Urbinus held out his cup to Rufus for more wine, and the young man filled it, moving more quietly than I would have expected he could with his build.

"No, we went up to the market afterwards. The new teacher from Antioch has arrived at the school of Simonides and he was supposed to be giving a dissertation; but it seems that the winds were contrary and the learned man was still recovering from his crossing. We walked twice round the old basilica and then came home."

"Why twice?" asked Urbinus, laughing.

"The first time for exercise, the second because something was happening at the Jewish meeting house and we wanted to see without staring. Nicolaus thinks it's vulgar to push about in a crowd."

"Did you find out what it was?"

"Not really. But it seems they have a new teacher there too—from Alexandria. I hope the sea was kinder to him. But it was a strange crowd, some of the shop people and the usual slaves, but there was the wife of a former councillor—I forget her name—there with the others."

"Strange, I hope there isn't going to be more trouble with them. The last time they had a new teacher there was nearly a riot and the case went to the proconsul," said Urbinus, suddenly the magistrate again.

It was not much longer before Nerea yawned twice and got up with a tired smile. Urbinus walked with her to the door. She turned there and said to me, "Timandra, will you see that all's well with Domina Olympias and then come to me? I think from now on we will have you sleeping in the little room next to mine."

39

I was glad of an excuse to see Olympias again. She was lying already curled for sleep against her high pillows, with only the tiny flame of a little lamp on the shelf above her bed casting a warm glow on her plume of hair. Rhodippe, the plump solemn girl who cared for her and had been born in the house, was folding clothes in the corner.

Olympias gave me a sharp look. "Well?"

I smiled, but could not think of anything to say that was not out of place from a slave.

"There is so much cruelty in our world," she said reflectively. "But there is even more stupidity and thoughtlessness, and that is no part of the plan of any god worth a pinch of incense. I think we are expected to have the common sense to deal with it ourselves, to leave space for the miracles where they are needed. I shall have an errand for you when you go to market, child, tomorrow or the next day."

3 · THE HOUSE OF TITUS

I had always lived in a city, with other families close on either side, their laughter and shifting of furniture only the thickness of a wall away, and outside the people who passed the doorway coming like the waters of a flood or a trickle as the sun rose and set. Even at mid-afternoon and midnight when the stream was at its lowest, there was always a dog barking away across the rooftops, or the distant hooves of a horse ridden fast that seemed, as one was jerked out of sleep by the sound, never to carry good news.

But the walls of the villa of the Torquartii were high and the noisy streets of the metal workers were far across the city. As I had passed the long days shut within the courtyards of the house I heard the sounds of our own kitchen or Nerea's cages of song-birds more often than the murmur of the city.

As the porter opened the gate for me two mornings later the noise outside made me flinch back. If Marcella, the kitchen girl who would carry my basket, had not been close behind, I do not think I would have been able to cross the threshold. Even with a thick veil to hide my face I felt uncovered as I turned right up the hill along the broad paved road that led to the market-place. When I had told Olympias that I wanted to walk out through a doorway it had been our own familiar gate at home that I had been thinking of, to run down the hill to the fountain between houses where everyone knew my name.

That walk became so familiar later, but the first time had the feeling of shock that comes from jumping into water that is colder than you had expected. After a while the strangeness began to wear off; I kept to the east side of the raised pavement, where the high roofs still cast a shadow to break the molten heat of the middle of the road. I knew there was not far to go, up this one road and then into the market to the small shops that Rufus had described to me. Nerea knew what she wanted but seemed strangely uncertain about where to buy it.

It was two hours after sunrise, children's chanting voices came from a high window, the corner food stalls were already busy, but it was too early yet for the ladies of the city to be out. A councillor came out of an imposing gateway across the road, followed by an eddy of clients and servants, but mostly I was jostled by errand boys and slaves going to market, and the road was choked with strings of pack-asses coming up from the harbour and carts going back the other way.

Then at a more open place where there was a drinking fountain and the small portico of a shrine, I looked up and saw the high crest of Acrocorinth, tawny-gold against the brilliant sky, an armed citadel above the high columns and statues of the gateway that led to the agora. Corinth was a Roman city, a colony, but the Roman temples and basilicas had been built by Greeks, and their proportions and the marble from which they had been made were Greek, even as I was myself. All the generations of Rome could not change that.

I went quickly through the dark tunnels of the gateway and stopped just inside, with my back to the base of a statue, to make certain where I was. The oblong space in front of me was full of people, living—or carved in marble and standing in stone in niches and on the many pedestals. Mostly the paved space in the centre was clear of stalls, the flower-sellers and the wreath-makers were spilling their roses and lilies out of the square doorways of the rows of shops that lined three sides of the market. Only on the far side, where in two places wide steps went up to a higher level, the last of a crowd of citizens in clean togas were making their way into the buildings that must house the law courts and the council house. It was an auspicious day and there was business to attend to.

The shops I was looking for were in a colonnade to my right, below a large temple with strong plain pillars that seemed to belong to a different age. I thought I must remember to ask Rufus what it was. Nerea had decided that she needed almond oil and new tweezers, poppy seed, squill bulbs and honey. At the counter of a linen merchant I bought red thread to finish the embroidery of a new dress and left orders for bales of wool to be taken to the villa so that Nerca could choose a new winter cloak for her husband. Everywhere I bargained carefully, partly because I had always had to be careful with money, and partly because I was spending now something that was not my own and if I was careless I might not be sent again.

I had finished in an hour and the basket was full. Nothing had been difficult, and the men lounging in the colonnade had made only the comments I had learned to deal with years before. Marcella was hot and yawning, and I would have liked to send her home ahead, but then I might have been in trouble. It is strange how two women who could do very little to help each other except scream twice as loud, always seem better protected than when they are alone.

There was now only my last errand, and this had been given me by Olympias. Face the eastern basilica, she had said and take the narrow street to your left. Go down the first on your right after the archway and look for a gate into a court-yard where the lintel is carved with a branched candlestick. The door you want is one beyond that. Marcella flopped down on a nearby doorstep while I knocked. It was quiet away from the busy market and cooler, for the high walls still kept the street in shadow. Far inside the house a man was singing, something with a repeated refrain. It sounded like part of the worship of a god, but not one I knew.

An old man answered the door to my knock. "I was to ask for the house of Titus," I said, feeling shy now.

"Titus Justus lives here," he said. "But my master will be away for an hour yet."

"I had a message. I was to ask him to remember the question that Domina Olympias Torquarta asked when he last came to the house on the Laechium road; and to say she was glad that she believed she need not wait much longer. It seems a strange message, can you remember it?"

"I have given messages like that before," he said, and I thought he had a kind face, unlike most porters I had seen before. "Go in peace, child."

The road home was downhill. When I had nearly reached the gate of the villa I thought for the first time that I could pass it and never see the household of Urbinus again. At any time since I had come out more than an hour before I could have given Marcella the slip, but if I had run away I might have got no farther than Chenchraea, and I would have left my father's burial place unvisited. Besides, Rufus had said on that first day that a slave once need not be a slave for ever. Already after a month the gate ahead seemed like "our" gate, one I should know for long years—as indeed I have— and besides I wanted to know if I had bought the right tweezers.

I had, and Nerea was pleased. She was sitting in the garden court where a vine trained over a trellis and a fig tree made a patch of shade over one of the marble benches that were set in the gaps of the colonnade. This was her place, near the door of her room, where she always sat in a bright clutter of cushions and embroidery silks with Pyrrha beside her in her cradle. I unpacked my purchases one by one and Nerea wrote down what I had spent on wax tablets hanging from her girdle. She was playing the careful housewife now, as if an economy over poppy seed could really help her husband meet the expenses of his magistracy.

The rest of the morning passed, and I was beginning to think it was time to fetch Nerea's midday meal when Hegiso's scolding voice sounded above the twittering Pyrrha was making. She came fussing into the garden followed by Dion, limping, with an arm round Rufus's shoulders. His sandal was half unlaced, and inside it his foot was wrapped in a bloodstained rag.

"Oh, Mistress, such a fright, and blood where the girls have just washed the floor, and me with the bread half risen out of the mixing bowl!"

"Then go back and see to it, please," said Nerea, not getting up. "Dion, is that foot badly hurt or just messy?"

His face was white but he managed some sort of a smile. "Mainly messy, I think. Don't worry, Nerea, it only needs bathing. Rufus will see to it."

"That was what I thought. Timandra, you know where my ointment box is; and fetch some of the old linen we tore up for the baby."

Dion limped into his room while I was fetching the things that were needed. When I came back he was sitting on the chest by his bed with Rufus squatting back on his heels inspecting the bloodstained foot.

"It's all coming from the split toenail, I think," he said. "Dip it in the water again, I can't see what I'm doing. It must have been a large stone you stubbed it on!"

Dion did not smile this time. He had started to shiver, as he sat with his head bent, watching the blood fan out into rusty spirals in the water. Rufus looked up and saw me, and I realized that he was puzzled. I looked round Dion's room—

I had not been in there before, but there was the usual collection of boy's things, special stones and a discus, some scrolls and a blanket woven with birds on the bed. I took down a thin cloak from a peg and put it round his shoulders; he pulled it closer without looking up.

"Timandra, can you tell if there's a bone broken?" asked Rufus.

I knelt down beside him and gently wiped the foot with a piece of rag. I was used to the knocks the sailors were always getting, and this looked painful but not serious—except for a boy with a race five days away. Perhaps this was why Dion seemed in such distress.

"No, I think it's only swollen," I said. "But it won't be fit to walk on again for two days. With a split nail it could easily turn poisoned." I reached for Nerea's ointment box and began to dress the toe. Dion held his foot steady on my knee and did not flinch when I pulled the bandage tight, but his hands gripped the chest, white-knuckled.

Rufus patted him awkwardly on the shoulder. "It may heal in time. If not there's next year!"

"If that was all that was wrong!" said Dion in a voice that he could not control. "What if anyone tells my brother that they saw me running out of the workshop of Asyncritas?"

"You were where?"

Dion could not answer, for he had turned round with his head on his arms and he was crying into his mattress. I remembered what Olympias had said about a small hurt soon being better than a larger one later. Then I saw from the look on Rufus's face that things were worse than that. I wanted to ask who Asyncritas was, but I dared not interrupt.

Rufus sat down on the far side of the bed, leant across, and touched the untidy hair. "Who took you there?" he asked.

I realized that he was old enough to have played with this youngest child of the house and spanked him when he needed it, for as long as Dion would be able to remember. What Dion had done must be told to someone and Rufus would hear the full story sooner alone. I tidied the water away and went outside, but not too far away.

When Rufus followed me out half an hour later his lopsided face was grave. He caught my eye and I followed him to the far end of the courtyard out of earshot of the main rooms.

"I'd better tell you, because you won't be as shocked as some people, and the women may start talking. If they do someone should know what to say. The young fool! The trouble is no elder brother has the authority of a father even if he is the head of the family. Also, friends can be one thing, but friends of friends something else. He can't help his looks, but if he can't someone should."

"But what happens at the workshop of Asyncritas?" I asked, still understanding nothing.

"Officially the manufacture of high class bronze statues and lamps and suchlike. The set in the dining-room came from there. In practice, although the man is an artist in his own way, only in a city like Corinth would he be allowed within speaking distance of the well-brought-up son of a citizen like Dion. But it happens that Nicolaus, who is older than he is, has a brother older still, with friends who delight in following all the less admirable habits of our ancestors, with a few from farther east added. Who do you think was the model when our lamps were made?"

I remembered the poised, naked athletes, their arms stretched high to lift the bronze lamp bowls. "You mean someone took Dion to the workshop to pose like that?"

"Something like. He says he didn't know what would happen, and there's a streak of innocence in him that makes it likely. He loves beautiful things; he only went to see where they were made. Then came the wine and compliments, and 'See the line of his neck, Asyncritas, the image of your

Drowsy Hermes!' But when they tried to demonstrate in greater detail, he woke up to what was going on. He knocked a statuette down on his toe as he was making his feelings quite clear! By then the artist had become very unpleasant and was thinking of using force not flattery."

"Oh, Rufus, what could have happened?"

"A memory that would make Dion sweat every time he thought of it. That's what he's understanding now, like someone looking over the edge of a cess-pit they've nearly fallen into, and feeling sick at the thought. He won't run in the games and he's probably lost a friend, and that will be punishment enough—unless it gets to the ears of the master. In some ways he's to blame that Dion is young for his age in such things, and I think he's beginning to see it at last. But this is one house in Corinth where there are strict moral standards, Domina Olympias has seen to that for sixty years. Urbinus and Secundus made their own discoveries and kept them to themselves, Dion doesn't understand living by two standards, so what are we to do about him? He honestly didn't know, Timandra, what he was about this morning!"

Some god must have given him his innocence for it to have lasted so long in Corinth, I thought. But it must have been an understanding god, because a Dion who was both good-looking and knowing would have been impossible to live in the same house with.

Dion was still in his room late that afternoon when the porter brought the news that Domina Olympias had a visitor. I had been hanging the baby's washing on the fruit trees in the kitchen garden, and ran back drying my hands on my tunic when I was called to attend the old lady. By the time I reached her room she had levered herself up in bed and her hair was standing up in even more amazing tufts than usual. I tidied her and tucked my own hair back under the scarf that covered it.

Olympias was bubbling with excitement, this visit must be one long hoped for. I did not know whom to expect when I went through to the atrium to fetch her guest, but it was not the man I saw waiting by the fishtank in the middle. Firstly, I knew he was not a citizen, for he wore a long robe of dark yellow linen which made his short curly hair and olive skin seem even darker by contrast; he was older than Urbinus, probably nearing forty, with the narrow, fine-boned face of a scholar. Father had carried enough of them from Athens to the Ionian coast for me to recognize the type. I could see as well that he was not pure Greek, and as I led him to Domina Olympias's room I was trying to work out where he came from, probably farther south and east than I had ever been.

"Peace be with you, and all in your house," he said, as my mistress gave him her dazzling smile of greeting. Then I had it, the accent was unmistakably Alexandrian.

"Apollos in my room on the very day that I send a message! That is a joy that brings me very great peace," she said. "Have you recovered from your journey, we heard that the winds have been contrary? Perhaps the walk here has made you thirsty?"

I had half risen from the stool by the door to which Olympias had waved me with an authoritative hand, but the man stayed me.

"No, I'm well, thank you." He looked at her for a long moment in silence. "Domina Olympias, you are just as I imagined you would be when our friend told me about the people I should meet in Corinth, those who would be like wells of water when I was weary from the desert of the city."

"Those who go through the valley of distress make of it a place of springs," she said, as if she was quoting something they both knew. "Now, did you bring me the book I was promised?"

"I did better, I brought you two. The hymns you asked for

49

and another which came into my hands unexpectedly—part of the first book of the law. It was with the writings which belonged to a brother who has just died in Ephesus; I brought it with my other scrolls, knowing I should find out who needed it now."

He reached into the breast of his robe and brought out two small scrolls. Olympias put out her hand, and then let it drop back on the bedcover; those fingers would never easily grip and unroll the parchment. The man Apollos moved more quickly than I could, as the excitement faded from the old woman's face; he sat down on the bed beside her as if he had been her son and unrolled the smaller scroll part way.

"Here's the one you particularly asked for." He pointed to the column of neat Greek script.

> *"Let the words that come from my mouth*
> *And the thoughts I ponder in my heart*
> *Be always fit for your eyes to see,*
> *My Lord, my rock, who redeems me,"*

she read.

"Domina Olympias, your eyes are keener than mine!"

"I'm used to the light in here, and that's one of my faculties at least that has been left me," she said rather crisply.

He let the scroll curl up on itself and went back to the chair by the bed. "Then you are well, truly well?" It seemed a strange thing to ask one so crippled, but before Olympias could answer a shadow fell across her bed.

Dion, in his undertunic and pale but tidy, was standing in the doorway, clearly perplexed by the unfamiliar face.

"No, don't go, Dion. You told me two days ago that you were interested in the arrival of a new teacher from Alexandria. Well, here he is, only the gossip of the market-place was a little stale, for Apollos has been some months in Ephesus." The man had turned in his seat to look gravely at the boy.

"This is my youngest grandson, and the one most likely to be interested in the books you have brought me."

Dion limped into the room and greeted Apollos politely although it was clear that the last person he wanted to talk to now was a stranger. He sat down on the edge of his grandmother's bed and picked up the other scroll.

He read for a moment and then looked up, puzzled. "Grandmother, I didn't know you were interested in the early philosophers?"

"Why do you say that?"

"Why, it's here, this must be Thales . . . 'And the spirit of God was moving over the face of the waters.' "

"Those words were old before the first of the seven sages was born, Dion," said Apollos. "Have you never seen the ancient writings of the Jews before?"

"No, but surely these . . ." He did not finish and his eyes went back to the written page.

The old woman and the man exchanged glances past his bent head. "These will be a great treasure, and I think I can be sure that Dion will read them with me too," said Olympias.

Apollos looked around him. "How long have you been here in this one room?"

"Ten, no, eleven years. Dion was five, I remember, the autumn when I had my second fall and the bones mended so badly. But you know I have always thought that there is no time in our lives when we can shut our minds and decide that we have stopped learning. Indeed the lessons of age are harder than most, but I think I have them by heart now. And this room grows bigger every month. Last month it was a whole new generation that came in when my great-granddaughter was brought to me for the first time. Now this month you have brought me a holy word from across the ages."

"And it was here that our friend came to you? You've never been to the house beside the synagogue?"

"No, never there, though before when I could travel in a litter I went to the synagogue itself and sat at the feet of the rabbi of that time. Esdras his name was, though you would never have heard of him, and a holy man as far as his light could guide him. I have much to thank him for. Now, where does it say 'I rejoice, my heart is ready. I will give thanks with the best member that I have'? "

"You will find it among the hymns, though I don't think you need to read them when you already know them so well by heart!"

"I intend to know them even better."

Dion stood up to go, still holding the scroll he had been reading.

"No," said his grandmother. "If you are going to bed early, and from your face that would be no bad thing, you may take the other scroll. I think the poetry in that will speak more directly to you tonight."

"I think that boy has the directness of mind to think for himself," said Apollos, after Dion had left the room.

"Perhaps. It may be because he's the youngest, and so was burdened earlier with grown-up talk and ideas," said Olympias. "There is no reason for me to hide from you what his future means to me."

"Then I'm glad that I saw him today."

"Yes, and I wouldn't have sent for him on your first visit, particularly as he is in distress and pain today. And it seems that I would have been wrong. It's reassuring to be overruled for the good of the very much loved."

"So this, other than the scrolls, was why you sent for me?"

She laughed, and it was not with the meaningless laughter of the very old. "You undervalue yourself, Apollos. Timandra, I think I can hear Pyrrha crying; by the time you have seen to her, my guest will probably be ready to leave."

There could be no impropriety in leaving so old a lady alone with a strange man, I thought, as I went out to soothe a crimson-faced baby. Still, I wondered what she wanted to talk about so privately, for I had already learnt that most freeborn people consider the slaves who attend them to be as deaf as statues.

That evening the sun set into an amber haze above the violet mountains at the end of the Gulf, and a small wind came off the water to revive the heavy air. Urbinus had come home early from the baths with a group of friends, so Nerea had dined alone in her room while they discussed business over their meal, and seemed likely to go on talking long after dark. Nerea was glad of the peaceful evening, for the baby still woke us both at nights, and her strength had not fully returned. Dion, too, had stayed in his room. The curtain over the doorway was looped partly back and the soft glow of his lamp shone out into the courtyard as I passed with the last of Pyrrha's herb-scented laundry in my arms.

Then I remembered the split toe. It probably needed dressing again and he would certainly not do it properly for himself; I had never been into his room before that day, but something stronger than the caution life with Hegiso was teaching me made me glance in quickly.

Dion was sitting on his bed with his tunic flopped down round his waist, slowly rubbing oil into his shoulder, and there was something in his face that was a louder cry for help than any words he could have spoken. I forgot about his bandaged foot.

"Can I help you?" I asked, saying the first thing that came into my head. "You can't reach round the back."

He looked up and seemed about to speak, and then I saw his mouth tremble and knew that if he spoke he would cry. I took the oil flask out of his hand and went round behind where I could not see his face; his shoulder and arm were grazed. As I smoothed the oil in I was thinking very quickly. In all the time I had so far lived in the house I had never imagined that someone like Dion could be lonely. But he had no brother near him in age and his parents dead, all the love and thought of Olympias could not make up to him for the lack of younger companionship. I had been sunk so deep in the tides of my own misery that I had seen no further than the urgent physical needs of my mistress and her child, and the solace of working my body hard so that my thoughts would be stilled by exhaustion. Besides, what relationship could there possibly be between the younger brother of the master and a woman slave beyond either the impersonal hands and feet to fetch and carry, or the early experimenting of a boy nearing maturity and looking for a convenient and docile girl. With his looks, I was probably the only one in the house who had not thought myself to sleep with a detailed picture of what that would be like.

I could not rub oil into his back for much longer, and I could feel that Dion was trembling again as he had in the morning. Then the night wind blew the lamp flame so that it flared, shooting black shadows across the walls and then dimmed to a bead of blue light as the wick slipped sideways in the oil. It became dark in the room.

"Timandra, were you a slave for long before my brother bought you?" Dion asked, his voice coming sudden and flat out of the concealing darkness.

"No, I was not. I was a freeborn captain's daughter, and then in five days my world tipped over and spilled me into the slaver's shed at Chenchraea."

"So you know how it feels?"

"Of course I do, women feel things as much as men."

"I never said they didn't." I was glad that I had annoyed him. "Then you can tell me what happens afterwards? After the world tips up. How do you go on? I feel as if I'm standing on the edge of a landslide with no way forward."

"You sleep and you wake, and after a little while you even begin to eat again, and your mind goes numb so that at first you only feel the little things—like an aching toe. Dogs go away and lick a sore place and stay quiet, but I don't think that's right for us. The gods have made us to fight our fate."

"What gods, Timandra? I wanted to run in honour of Poseidon of the Sanctuary. Do you think he refused me because I was unworthy or because he was indifferent?"

I would have liked to tell him to stop being dramatic about a god who would have meant little to him if his temple had not stood on the Isthmus of Corinth. As a sailor's daughter I knew more about the worship of Poseidon than he ever would. He was being silly but I would be no help to him if he thought I was unsympathetic. There was no time for me to be surprised at how much I wanted to help.

"Dion, why don't you go to bed? I know you think you won't sleep. Very well, read your grandmother's scroll all night if you can get that lamp to burn properly. That's better than sitting in the dark being miserable, at least your body will be resting. Try not to think about your friend and what he's going to say when he comes to see you tomorrow as I expect he will. You think you've made a fool of yourself, but he's probably ashamed too, and you may need to say nothing. As for the race, you haven't broken your leg, and there's always next year. Be thankful you haven't got to lie for months with the prospect of it setting wrong and crippling you for life."

"So Rufus told you what happened this morning."

"Yes, it sounded horrible."

Suddenly he leant back against me in the dark in a companionable way, and I felt the warmth of his bare shoulder through the thin linen of my tunic; and he did not seem like a young man who might wither my heart with fear, but someone young and puzzled like myself. And I had called him by his name, without thinking, as one does to a friend.

Then I heard his nice, boy's laugh. "All this over a split toenail! You're right, I think the best thing to do would be to go to bed properly and read. My grandmother has some strange friends; I remember there was a time when a constant procession of philosophers and teachers came and went in her room. I suppose it was after she was crippled, though I was too young at the time to understand that might be the reason. She must have been searching for her firm ground, or new gods after her world tipped up. I never thought to ask her what she found."

He stood up and stretched hugely, and as I trimmed the lamp wick I thought he would not read as long as he expected that night, but that this was only the first round in a long contest and there would be other fights ahead.

4 · SECUNDUS

Dion's toe healed well and caused him very little trouble after the first two days, and by then he was friends with Nicolaus again as I had expected, although I never heard what they said when they met again for the first time. I suppose it was partly their unlikeness that had attracted them to each other; Nicolaus was thin, dark and sardonic, the son of a lawyer, and Dion quoted his cleverness to the family until they must often have been sick of the sound of his name, except that Dion's enthusiasms were very infectious.

Around the middle of the month Secundus, the second brother, came home again. I believe Urbinus had something to do with his transfer to the staff of the proconsul; he certainly found him very useful for the rest of the summer. However, Secundus arrived home on one hot night in a bad humour, and for me the trouble began at once.

It had been another of the evenings when Nerea was alone and had gone to bed early. Long after the kitchen fire had been covered for the night and most of the household had gone to bed, we heard the sounds of an arrival and Nerea sent me to find out what was happening. I found the young man standing in the atrium wrenching at the straps of his helmet, while the porter carried in his equipment. His face was red and sweaty in the lamplight, and he had already thrown his cloak down over the rim of the fish tank so that the hem was trailing in the water. As there was no one to greet the son of the house except me I went forward and began to unbuckle the stiff straps of his armour. It looked like a new suit, ornamented for ceremonial occasions, but probably heavy and not yet worked comfortable. That might explain why he looked so bad-tempered.

He stood, fidgeting and humming through his teeth, till I had finished, and then strode through into the garden courtyard where the family rooms were. I left someone else to collect his scattered belongings and ran to the kitchen for wine in one of the best cups.

When I brought it to Secundus he was sprawling across the marble bench under the fig tree where a hanging lamp left burning for Urbinus's return still made a pool of light. Olympias's room was in darkness and Nerea had let the curtain fall back across her door.

"My brother's out?" he asked.

"Yes, we didn't expect you today."

"I was suddenly bored with Athens, and my new mount made short work of the journey. Jupiter Ammon! I suppose if Urbinus is out Rufus is with him, and I've been promising myself his attentions ever since I crossed the Isthmus Causeway, with the baths shutting at dusk. That'll have to wait. Bring me a bowl of water here."

I went to fetch the shallow bronze bowl Nerea used, and a ewer of water. This was not part of my usual work, for Rufus usually attended the men of the family, but there seemed no help for it. I was certain that Hegiso would not appear until the messy work was done.

Secundus splashed water over his face and neck while I held the basin, and then sat back holding a second cup of wine while I knelt to bathe his feet. I felt his eyes pass carelessly over me as I bent over my work. His legs were long and brown, and even without the moulding of his breastplate his body had the hard muscles of long training; his features were regular and handsome and his thick hair still lay close to his head from the weight of his helmet. He had his older brother's dark colouring and was like him in some ways, but there was something missing; he had neither Dion's grace nor Urbinus's seriousness.

"Now, who are you exactly?" he asked, leaning back and looking at me under his dark lashes as I got up to empty the water.

"Timandra of Samos," I said. "The master bought me after Prisca died."

"Bring me some more wine then, Timandra of Samos."

I brought him the jug this time, already mixed, and he sat there drinking while I tidied away the towels. My mind was running ahead to what food was left in the kitchen after Nerea's supper, and to his bed not made up. He showed no signs of moving when I went across to the storeroom to fetch sheets and a bedcover. I lit a lamp from the stand in the courtyard and carried it to his room; my mind was busy with the changes his coming would make in the household when a shadow fell across the partly made bed.

Secundus stood in the doorway with a hand on each doorpost. "Aren't you lonely minding the house alone in the evenings, Timandra of Samos?" he asked.

I could not see his face clearly, but I knew that the wine he had just drunk had not been his first that evening. I could smell the sweetness of it as I pulled the cover smooth and made to pass him, my face frozen into an artificial calm.

"Where are you going now?" he asked, clutching at my shoulder as I passed, and turning me with my back against the wall.

I did not try to pull away, but stood still while his hot fingers fumbled with the clasps at the shoulder of my tunic, trying to find a way through to the skin. "I can't get you a pillow if you don't let go of me."

"What do we want with pillows . . . Timandra?"

His eyes had widened like those of a small boy who sees a sticky sweet suddenly within his reach.

"Leave me alone." I raised my voice only a little, but my tone made him pause. He really thinks I want to undress and lie down on the bed with him, I thought. He can't imagine any reason I might have for not wanting to!

He tried to pull me closer. The wine smell made me feel sick, and it was a smell that meant fear to me. I drew my elbows in close against my body and pushed hard against his chest. It was like trying to move a rock. Now fear was really on me, for I would have to help myself. I struck upwards with my knee and then wrenched quickly sideways. Secundus loosed his hold, grunting more with anger than with pain, for I had not dared to hit too hard. He was after me across the courtyard before I was half-way to Nerea's room.

I had forgotten Dion. He had been so quiet during the last few days that I was often not sure if he was in or out. Now he came suddenly into the lamplight. Secundus's tunic was twisted and his face flushed, and my hair had come down.

"Greetings, brother," said Dion. "I see you are making yourself very much at home. Go to bed, Timandra, I'll see to any further entertainment that seems needed."

I went into the small room where Pyrrha was already asleep as if I was a scolded child. It was dark there and quiet, with only the occasional small sounds of the sleeping baby, and a faint glow shining across on to the rough white walls above my bed from a crack in the curtains. I dared not cry because Nerea might still be awake.

I lay rigid on my bed, with my shift loose against my hot skin except where it touched the hard mattress and there it clung stickily. Flies droned against the walls and even in here there was no coolness. I turned on one side to let the air get to the sweat-damp linen, and pushed the loose hair out of my eyes.

SECUNDUS

My fingers closed on a hard roundness under my pillow, a smooth grey pebble, eggshaped and streaked with white lines. It fitted, cool and familiar, into the palm of my hand, and I lay more quietly, soothed by the memory of a sandy beach between two headlands a morning's ride from home, where I had played as a child. Behind it in a fold in the valley lay my grandfather's farm, a memory of welcome and new smells and fresh winds to a child from the small city who came only at harvest time and for the great family festivals. As my fingers stroked the stone I thought of the child who had run across sand which burnt her feet, to the edge of calm water, turning from blue to emerald out where it was deeper beyond a little island. The mountains of Ionia that lay east across a narrow channel had seemed near enough to touch.

As I lay, too tired and full of misery to sleep, the memory of Samos and a child's sandy hand reaching through the ripples for a shining stone seemed too distant to hurt me any more. The wet stone had dried dull, and now I had been two months in Corinth, and before that the months since my mother's death had loosened the hold my old home had for me. Nerea, who had always lived beneath the acropolis at Corinth, would not be able to understand how the web of custom that binds a woman to one city and one hill could ever loosen. But my life had been wrenched out of its frame like a web torn roughly from a loom. Now, when the cobweb-thin threads which would weave me back into security were beginning to form again, Secundus had come crashing through them with clumsy hands. I had given wise advice to Dion, but I could only stifle my own crying in my pillow, while the grey stone grew warm in my hand.

In the morning I woke with a heavy head as one often does after a miserable night, Pyrrha was fretful and Nerea had woken with backache and seemed to want nothing except to be left alone in a darkened room. By the time they were both settled the sun was well up, but it was veiled by high cloud and the courtyard was filled with a dull glare that made my headache worse. I went through into the kitchen courtyard with my daily basket of the baby's washing.

Hegiso was talking to the gardener while he cut lettuces for her. She watched me coming with her hands on her hips; I could tell she was pleased about something, but my mind was working so slowly that morning that I did not guess that it could be anything to do with me.

As I went to pass her she put out a fat hand and swung me back.

"So now we know what the lady from Samos is like, after all!" she said to the gardener, who sniggered obligingly. "Flesh and blood like the rest of us."

I tried to pull away, because her hand was hot and sweaty.

"I saw you, Timandra. There was not much light but I saw you with the young master, and him not half an hour in the house!"

"If you saw me with Secundus you could have helped me with his bed," I said, and I think my voice was quiet but I could not keep it from shaking.

"Not the sort of help you were giving him, and me a decent woman and forty years in this house," she said, with a sneer that brought down a red flood of rage before my eyes that I fought to keep back. "Harbour sweepings you are, not fit to wait on a nice lady like ours, and I'm surprised that the master can't see it for himself. Still, there's those that can tell him!"

I pulled free and ran back into the courtyard, fighting down the stream of ugly, bitter words that I had almost screamed back at her. Hegiso would not listen or understand a justification, and she would not forget a single word that I said against her; I would pay for such words one by one, a weary day at a time. I must learn to bear her misunderstanding. Through the farther archway I could see Nicolaus waiting, and Dion was just coming out of his room. He paused and came back when he saw me.

"Whatever is it?" he asked, for I was trembling and speechless, with my head thundering and tears running down my cheeks. "Is it Secundus last night? Don't worry, he's like that sometimes, but he won't try twice or he knows I'll tell Urbinus. I know you couldn't help it."

"But Hegiso says she saw . . ." I sniffed hard and dried my eyes on the fold of my tunic, but my nose was running.

"What could she see, nothing happened?"

"She'll invent then. What if she tells the master? Why should he believe me instead of her, after she's been so long in the house?"

"I would have thought he'd remember the way she told tales when we were children, but he does have a habit of not listening to problems when things go wrong at home." He sounded less certain now. Nicolaus called impatiently from the atrium.

"I must go, why don't you talk to Grandmother, you know how soothing she is? I'll help if I can. I promise. You were good to me."

He gave me an encouraging smile and ran off to join his friend. Again I felt walls close round me as the door shut behind the two of them and left me inside the house.

I turned to go into Olympias's room, for Dion had been right, she was the one person in the house who would be certain to understand and be sympathetic; but before I could reach the door I heard Pyrrha crying, and then Nerea calling my name.

My mistress had raised herself up on one elbow and was gazing distractedly at the crimson-faced baby in the cradle.

"Do stop her making that noise, it goes straight through my head. Is she ill?"

I picked her up. Her swaddling bands were wet and her eyes were so tight shut that the tears could hardly get out.

"I expect she fed too fast. Greedy girl!" The howls subsided as I rubbed the baby's back, and Nerea sank down against her pillows. I sat on a stool, for Pyrrha had been large at birth and she was still heavy for her age.

Nerea lay with her eyes closed, her dark hair sticking in damp curls round her forehead. The summer sun of Corinth beat down on the courtyard outside, but the room was shaded and cool, quiet except for the twitter of cage birds outside in the colonnade. I wondered if all was well with Nerea or if this was the beginning of a fever. With Hegiso in her present mood I did not know how I should manage if my mistress were ill.

Pyrrha's eyes closed too and she settled into the curve of my arm. I laid her down in the cradle and went through into the small room next door to put away the clean linen I had brought in from the garden. Being with the baby had calmed me, as it always did, for the way I could quiet her and that she throve in my care was the one steady growing thing in my life in the last months; Olympias and Dion had been kind to me, but Pyrrha I loved, for it would be years yet before she understood that I was a slave. For the moment I had forgotten Hegiso's threats, till I heard her voice next door through the curtain between the rooms.

"I saw her with my own eyes, my lady, with the master's brother. Now that's never been the way in this household, not Rhodippe or any of the other girls, and none of the young masters ever before. It's clear the girl brought her harbour ways into the house with her. . . ."

Nerea's voice was tired and shrill. "Oh, Hegiso, not now. What can I do about it? You must speak to the master when he comes home."

"But I'm not easy about it, my lady, I'm not easy about it

at all; with the girl always about you and our dear baby. If a girl isn't honest one way what chance is there that she's honest in others?"

"Hegiso, please, my head's so bad!"

"It's you I'm thinking of, my lady, it was a bad day when she came into the house. And Timandra up to the market most days. How do we know what she takes out of the house?"

That was too much, for Hegiso's words could be threatening my small, precious freedom sometimes to leave the villa. I pushed the curtain aside and went through into the other room.

Hegiso's face went brick-red. Her mouth opened and shut, then she waddled to the door before making her parting remark. "I told you she had nasty ways, my lady!"

Nerea looked really feverish by now. I poured water into a bowl so that I could bathe her hands and face, but I was trembling and splashed some on the marble floor. Nerea let me make her comfortable and then opened her eyes as I still bent over her, with my hand on her hot forehead.

"Timandra, why did you make Hegiso so cross with you? Now there will be no peace for days, and I feel so ill. You should know by now that she's stupid, and sees and tells more than she should."

"But, my lady, I've done nothing for her to tell anyone about!"

"Oh, what does that matter? And we were getting on so well, and since the baby was born she's been much less tiresome than she was when I was first married. Now leave me quiet, I want to sleep before it gets too hot."

She closed her eyes and turned over on her side while I stood staring down at her, speechless. I did not know whether to be more surprised that she believed what Hegiso had told her, or that she only minded because it threatened to disturb the peace of the household.

Olympias was sitting up in bed looking down at a scroll which had slipped off the covers and on to the floor. I picked it up and gave it back to her; it was one of the two the teacher, Apollos, had brought a few days before. From the other end of the courtyard came the sounds of Hegiso shouting at the kitchen girl and banging brass pots about.

"I think the house is not happy this morning," Olympias said. "It was listening to the very familiar sounds of Hegiso beginning one of her rages that made me drop my book." She peered at my face perceptively. "You also are not a placid person, Timandra, and today you are strung up like an over-tuned lyre. I think Secundus is being troublesome again."

"Again, Grandmother?"

"Yes, certainly again. I have been telling him ever since he was sixteen that if no code of ethics could help him to contain himself he should arrange for his entertainment outside the house. I will not have our girls molested. But it has had very little effect; he was always Hegiso's pet, she spoiled him when he was a baby and she still makes trouble when he's here."

"I didn't really mind what she said, it didn't hurt because we don't like each other anyway. It was what my mistress said; she didn't seem to mind if it was true or not as long as it wasn't a nuisance."

Olympias looked at me very kindly. "Now sit quiet while I think."

She lay back and I sat on a stool to wait. Already I felt quieter, not because of anything she had been able to do but only because she had understood.

Her eyes were suddenly open again and looking at me. "Timandra, I think you are a girl who needs to understand before you can trust; you don't find it easy to be faithful in the darkness."

It was a statement, not a question, I dropped my eyes from hers.

"Now, you understand Hegiso and Secundus only too well, but you could not possibly understand Nerea unless you knew, for example, that she has not left this house since she was married."

"Never once? But how long is it—fifteen, sixteen months?"

"Never once, and before that she had not left her father's house since she was a little girl."

"What had happened? Was she ill?"

"Yes, I think so, but not with a sickness many people would recognize. She has never talked to me about it, but Prisca, who died before you came to us, had been with Nerea since she was a baby and she told me what I know. Now you were used to going about freely at home, weren't you; to the market with your mother or down to the harbour to wave goodbye to your father's galley? You even sailed with him for short trips. You still enjoy being free of the house for an hour when you can, don't you?"

"Yes, of course."

"There would be no 'Of course' for Nerea, for she has never been free like that. Her father is the priest of Jupiter for this city, and although perhaps the customs were a little different in Samos you will know what that means. Even here we do not follow the observances as strictly as in Rome, but the life of such a man is closely regulated and bound by prohibitions, and Nerea's father takes his priesthood very seriously—it has run in his family since the refounding of the city. Death and illness are always kept hidden from that household as far as possible; it was a very protected life for a treasured child. Then one day, this little girl, dressed in a new tunic, is taken on a promised visit to an aunt. Prisca said it was like the impracticality of her master not to remember that the death sentence on three robbers was due to be carried out that day. It was an ill chance that took the litters on the road past the gallows."

"The child saw that?"

"Two men newly crucified, strung tight and bloody, and the other stripped and struggling. Prisca had Nerea in the litter with her, and the curtains were drawn, but the child heard men yelling and peeped out. I think that was the last thing she ever saw beyond the walls of these two houses. She screamed till she was sick, and then she fainted. The litters turned back and a doctor was called but he could only watch over her while she wilted with fever like a flower in the hot sun. Then she seemed to recover herself and became the quiet child she had been before—unless they tried to take her out of the house. They only tried twice."

"But what happened when she was married?"

"At the time of course no one knew more than that Urbinus's bride was young and shy. But you see, her mother was ill by then, though Nerea knew nothing of it, and I think she realized there would soon be a death in the house despite all she could do. They brought the girl here in a curtained litter, probably partly drugged so that she hardly understood. Her mother died a month later, so she did not see her again."

I was appalled by what I had heard—that a young life could be so warped by parents who were trying to be kind. In what distorted way did my mistress understand life when this was all that she had seen of it?

"Why have you told me?" I asked.

"Because although you are impatient now, one day you may be wise, and also I need your help. Nerea's happiness is as delicately balanced as an acrobat standing on his hands. I don't know how she came through the shock of Prisca's death and her own confinement, but she has learnt over the years to be very skilful in drawing the shutters over her mind when something happens that she cannot bear or understand. However, she is still far from well, and you must not expect her to understand your problems although she will never mean to be unkind."

I stood up, feeling grave and a little sick as I tried to understand what Olympias had told me. "But is there no way that she can be healed from this, Grandmother?"

"There are ways and I have ... thought," she stumbled for the word, "long and hard about it, but the time hasn't been right. It is beyond the skill of an ordinary doctor to go back into the wounded mind of the child who is still there inside the woman my grand-daughter has become. Yet till that is done Nerea is in prison, and it may be that you can help to free her. Don't talk about this to anyone."

"Does no one else know about it?"

"Dion has seen the edge of something he does not understand, Urbinus is grateful for a quiet and submissive wife. It is not easy for a man to understand what is beyond human understanding."

She closed her eyes as if in dismissal, and I tiptoed away from the bed, but before I had reached the door she called me back.

"Now there is something I have forgotten. Oh yes, the reason why I was telling you all this in the first place. I don't often need to speak firmly to Hegiso now, after all the years we have known each other we understand very clearly where there are cracks in the pavement that we must walk around. Don't be afraid of Urbinus; if he should hear what happened last night I promise you it will not be from her, and only from her could it do you harm. You are fortunate in that this house is ruled by the moral code of my eldest grandson; some behaviour and some of the easy assumptions made by the young men of a city like Corinth he will not tolerate, and he knows Secundus very well. I think it makes up for the times when he is blind to the small things that disturb us, shut up in the house together as we are, that he sees the larger things very clearly indeed."

5 · THE MARKET-PLACE

There had been guests to dinner, important men, so we had been busy all day putting clean covers on the cushions and polishing the furniture in the summer dining-room. The salt wind from the gulf tarnished the bronze lamps and had scattered the limp rose petals almost as soon as they were arranged.

I was aching all over with weariness by the time the last guest went, but not quite as sleepy as I had been an hour before. If Rufus had not jogged me with his elbow then I should probably have dozed on my feet, as we stood waiting to refill the wine cups when the main eating was over. By then the room was heavy with the smell of cooling meat and dying flowers, and the low hum of serious conversation sounded like bees in a hayfield. Even the wind that blew out the thin curtains and sent wave shadows across the painted walls was warm and stale.

When the house was quiet I still could not go to bed, because Pyrrha, woken by the guests making noisy goodbyes outside Nerea's room, would not settle. Then Urbinus came in and gave me the nod that meant he wanted to talk to his wife in private. He looked grave and I thought she was scared, so I picked the baby up and walked heavily through to the far terrace, splashed with sharp leaf shadows from the vine that grew on the trellis above.

I thought the wind had dropped, but then another gust came with a noise over the olive groves below the town like a long wave breaking on the shore. It turned the shadows to ripples over water, and it was so beautiful and I was so tired that I wanted to cry, as Pyrrha settled heavier in sleep against my shoulder.

Another shape moved against the brightness of the three-quarter moon. Dion spoke without looking round.

> *"The heavens tell the glory of God,*
> *The sky proclaims his work.*
> *Day speaks to day,*
> *And night tells knowledge to night."*

"I know," I said, "I remember thinking that once before. It was last year, the only other time I sailed this far with Father. And the words were the same too."

"What words, how could they have been?"

He spoke so sharply that I was surprised. "Why, where do they come from that I couldn't have heard them?"

"I'm sorry, it was just strange. I found them in one of the hymns in the book Grandmother lent me, only there was a lot more."

"Then it must have been the rabbi last year! We took him from Chenchraea to Ephesus; there were four passengers, all friends, and one of them with a wife. I remember her because she was kind to me. I had a boil on my neck and she dressed it for me. We sailed from here at night, the moon was so bright, and I couldn't sleep. That was when I talked to the rabbi."

"Tell me about it," said Dion.

"Don't you want to go to bed?" I asked. I was longing for sleep myself, but I knew it was too soon to go back, and that talking here quietly was a treat that would not happen often, with the darkness to make it easier.

"No, I've eaten too much and heard things I didn't understand. But don't be frightened, I'm not drunk!"

"I didn't think you were," I said, laughing, and settled Pyrrha down into my lap. "It wasn't that anything very exciting happened, only a night when the moon woke me and I got up to see it set. It wasn't long before dawn and it was hanging low in the east like dark polished brass—as if it was a dying sun. Then the sky started to get brighter and brighter, but then nothing else happened, and as I sat in the bows I thought that perhaps this once the true sun wouldn't rise at all, because it was so long in coming."

"I know that feeling, when everything seems to wait and hold its breath."

"Yes, that was what the man said; I wish I could remember his name. The sea was very still, like a grey veil with the wrinkles smoothed out, and it seemed to go up all the same colour until it turned into the twin peaks of Salamis and the mountains behind on the mainland. There were some little clouds just starting to turn a rusty pink and as I watched them a voice said, 'I think this is the longest hour of the day.' And I said, 'No, it's the hour after midnight if you can't sleep.' And I didn't even turn round, because it was just like the other part of my mind speaking. It was then that he said the words you were saying now, about the day and night talking, and I wanted to ask him which god he thought had made them. Then the sun suddenly seemed to jump into the sky and the air went gold and he said something else."

"More words from the book? I wonder if I can guess. It's beautiful, Timandra, and I've read some of it so often that I know it by heart now. Yet it gives me a strange feeling because to me it's poetry but there is a warning in the words that to the people who wrote them they meant something very much more important. Listen. . . .

The first councillors burst out and scattered like ruffled chickens; they were mostly old men and the guards let them go. But behind them was an escort and the dishevelled figure of a tall man under guard, the heavy folds of his toga slipping and muffling him as though they were grave bands. Then even from across the market I saw red stains on his shoulder where blood dripped from a smeared wound on his brow. There were other men behind being hustled out but he was the one the crowd knew; they flowed forward as far as the cordon would let them, but the soldiers had their javelins ready to push or stab.

Then I saw that the narrow streets leading into the market were suddenly full. I turned to go back but the gateway was already blocked. There was a flower stall in the angle of the wall behind me. As the noise began again I pushed back to it; the market woman was frantically lifting down her jars and baskets and storing them under the trestles. She knew what was going to happen. I got an arm round the pole of her awning, and my feet on an upturned jar, and then I could see all too clearly.

Shouting like that I had heard before, for no excited crowd can keep quiet long; but then it was suddenly different. The wounded man had been taken almost to the end of the upper terrace but there he stopped and turned to the people as if he wanted to make a speech. Half the mob hushed to hear him, but the rest made a strange sound, a yowl like a mob of hunting cats and then a regular pulsing chant, mindless and evil. It must have been the noise the crowd make in the amphitheatre when a gladiator falls.

The guarded man knew it, he was turning away when an eddy swept across the market and I saw tossing helmet plumes. A squad were forcing their way through the crowd with two boys of about ten and twelve and an old man in their midst. Behind them were three slaves tightly bound. The man saw them and seemed to sag and grow smaller while I watched, but he was pulled away even before they reached the steps.

At one end of the market an arcade with small shops was still being built. It was from the workmen who hung like a great garland from the scaffolding that the first stones came. They seemed to be aimed at the other councillors who were now thronging out and down the steps. As the guard sloped javelins and moved forward I remembered Urbinus and tried to find his face, but the stall was beginning to rock wildly as the crowd pressed back, most of them trying to flee into the protection of the streets.

Hands grabbed me and pulled me down. As I stumbled off balance I was shaken and righted and Dion hissed in my ear, "Drop that basket and follow close."

His hand kept tight hold of my wrist, pulling me behind him. I no longer knew any more than my ears could tell me of what was happening, but he seemed to know where he was making for and that forced him across the current of a crowd running blindly. The shutters were all up on the lower shops. He turned sharply up a narrow stair at the end of a row that led to an upper arcade. A fat merchant coming down blocked the way. We squeezed flat against the wall and I felt his trembling and heard his terrified wheezing as he pushed past. Above there were fewer people. Dion hammered on a pair of closed shutters and shouted a name. They were opened wide enough for us to slip through and then crashed shut behind us.

It was the workshop of a bookseller and copyist, a short fat Greek who seemed to know Dion well. It was dark now with the shutters closed, except at the back of the shop where a high window cast a beam of dusty light on the desks of the copying slaves, five of them huddled together with their pens still in their hands.

"Young master, we couldn't see. Was it Vipsanius Nerva?"

asked the Greek. The shouting below grew louder, there was a grinding crash, and then the noise seemed to change to something more uncertain.

"Yes, Pallas. This has been coming all summer, but today I suppose it was the usual charge of treason against the Emperor. Gallio was never one to be subtle."

Pallas made a warning face, for the slaves were listening, and Dion's lips tightened; he looked harassed and older. The little man left us and went to the back of the shop and Dion leaned against the counter.

My legs gave way and I sat on the customer's stool. "I did try to warn you," said Dion. "But I wasn't even sure it would be today. In an hour it should be safe to go home unless anyone starts burning things."

"But I still don't understand. Was that man with the cut head Vipsanius who came to dinner last month?"

"The leader of the progressive members of the council, the man who said the city needed a new aqueduct? Yes, I suppose it was about a month ago—before Urbinus saw how things were going, that any plan which needed money would never be agreed by the proconsul. He wants to take a full tax chest back to Rome with him when he's recalled."

"And now what's happening?"

"Vipsanius will be awaiting trial before an irregular court presided over by the proconsul on a charge of treason. It may take place today if his slaves are afraid of torture and one of them can think of something his master said that is sufficiently compromising. I hope for their skins that they do; they can't save him. I expect tomorrow he will be given the chance to commit suicide. Don't look at me like that. I don't know what else he's done—the other reasons why he suddenly became dangerous to know. Last month Urbinus was talking about marrying me to his daughter as soon as I'm of age."

"This autumn?"

"In Rome I could have been married at fifteen! I'm glad I wasn't, and it's lucky things hadn't gone very far. Poor child, I think Vipsanius saw clear enough ahead to send her on a visit to relations some days ago."

"Were those his sons in the market-place?"

"Where? I didn't see. I'd noticed you and I was trying to work my way round under the arcade before the trouble started. Listen, it's quieter now; Secundus's boys are efficient. We were afraid there would be a riot because Vipsanius was popular in some quarters, and I suppose some of his friends organized that stone throwing, but all they did was get men killed."

"In Samos when I was a little girl something like this happened, but we were kept in the house and I didn't understand," I said.

"And these are days of peace under the good Emperor Claudius, a scholar! How anyone stayed alive and harvested crops after the death of the first Caesar, with the war galleys of Antonius cruising up one coast and Pompeius down the other, I don't know." He laughed suddenly and bent forward to peer through a knot hole in the shutters. Feet ran past and then it was unnaturally quiet.

"What is it?" I asked.

"Nothing, the last of the guard, I'll slip out in a moment and have a look."

"No, I meant why did you laugh."

"Oh that, I was thinking about last night and that Jewish hymn. It seems a long time ago."

It was midday before Dion led me home by a back way through the alleys behind the Laechium road. Most of the shops still had their shutters up, but the cooking stalls were beginning to open again cautiously, with small knots of men talking about chariot teams or harbour news, anything except politics.

Nerea was prostrate and in tears, for Urbinus had reached home before us and she knew we must both be dead among the tumbled bodies and scattered stones that still lay near the partly collapsed scaffolding in the corner of the market-place. Hegiso only grumbled because I had lost the shopping basket.

Urbinus looked grave and his face was hard. I wondered as I looked at him why he, one of the four magistrates, was not at the council house. Then I remembered that he probably knew very well what he was doing, and understood his worried consultation with Nerea the night before. What power did he or any of the council have after all, when Rome stretched out one finger to move over the pieces on the gaming board? He took Dion away to the far terrace, which was the most private part of the house, for now that the first danger was over the boy had a hurt, lost look. During the last month, since he had injured his foot, he had turned very much to his brother and an interest in the affairs of the city. He was a boy who needed a passion, an overriding purpose, as I did myself. I sat for the rest of the afternoon in the room of Olympias wondering if he could ever find it this way.

Over the next few days I noticed that the old lady was less well than she had been. It was not that she had a fever, or anything with a name, only that the weight of age that hung about her like a cloak seemed to have grown heavier. She was very tired and yet she lay sleepless for long hours in the night. Being Olympias she did not complain, for if she had no strength to be pleasant she preferred to stay silent. However, I knew that I was not the only person in the household to see that she was already much weaker than she had been when Pyrrha was born. Only Urbinus, so much away these days in a city that seemed determined to be normal again, to pretend the trial and the riot had never happened, seemed not to understand.

I was sewing one afternoon in her room, sitting near the

door so that the late sun could fall on my work. I could feel the sweat stand on my body even with the effort of breaking the thread; swallows were calling and swooping across the court-yard outside and I could hear Nerea playing with her baby under the fig tree. The city noises were very far away, and in the quiet room Olympias had not moved for more than an hour. As I looked up from time to time I noticed that one of the scrolls that Apollos the teacher had brought was lying in the folds of the bedcover. I remembered again the words that Dion had quoted on the night of the party and for the first time I minded badly that I could not read them for myself.

When I looked up again her eyes were open and she was watching me more acutely than she had for some time, with the veil of a slightly distant sweetness drawn back.

"Why did you frown?" she asked.

"I was wishing I could read."

The bunched fingers moved to touch the scroll.

"Yes, that particularly. Grandmother, there are hymns to a god in it, aren't there? But how could one god be big enough to make the world, not the way it is in the old stories with gods and goddesses coupling and giving birth to winds and snakes that made everything. The Romans have little gods for every street corner and every grove of trees—they couldn't have joined together to make the sun and the sky, and if they had why should they care about us and the small offering we can give them?"

"You want a god who cares about small people?"

It seemed that my mind had suddenly fallen into darkness, and I was alone in it except for the sobbing of all the women I had ever heard weep. "How can we live if the gods don't answer? The family of Vipsanius Nerva will have offered a cake every day to the household gods, and now both husband and wife are dead by their own hands. And my father's offer-ings, what did they do for him? Are we quite alone in the world with nothing to save us from each other? I don't see how I can live like that, month after month wading forward with nothing firm under my feet. No family, nothing to hope for, only Hesigo shouting and people around me I haven't chosen. Is there no god for slaves, who can make slavery a way that we can live and not be quite forsaken?"

Then when I had spoken I was afraid, for Olympias had shut her eyes again and was lying very still. In my pain I had not thought of her, and now I had hurt her. I stood up quickly, dropping my sewing on the floor, and went over to the bed. I took one of her hands in both of mine; the twisted fingers clasped me and she opened her eyes with such a look of joy in them that I glanced quickly behind me, thinking that some-one else must have come into the room.

"Don't look so surprised," she said. "I've waited five years for someone to say that to me, and I was beginning to believe it wouldn't happen in time."

"But I thought I'd upset you!"

"Never that! Timandra, I don't know why you thought you spoke like that, but do you really want to know the answer? What would it be worth to you?"

I thought for only a moment before answering with sudden certainty. "My life, because if there are no gods what is it worth—nothing to me or anyone else!"

"Yes, you have the spirit to say that, but how if the cost was not one grand gesture, but something that seemed at first small and even silly?"

"A mystery, do you mean?"

"Yes, but not something confusing made up of strange rites. One of those simple, obvious things that people look at and don't see."

"You mean you know the answer? I suppose you must do, I never thought. Something that . . ." I stopped, not wanting to speak of her long agony of patience in a crippled body.

"Timandra, Nerea would let you leave the house in the evening if I sent you and someone was with you?"

"Yes, I expect so if Pyrrha was well. But where?"

Before she could answer Rufus stood in the doorway, waiting for permission to come in.

"My lady, there is a man, a teacher, asking for you. He says he has been before and that his name is Apollos. But are you well enough to see him?"

Again the look of joy flooded over Olympias's face so that for a moment the age seemed to leave it. "Timandra, straighten the covers. Really it is so much easier receiving gentlemen now that it doesn't matter how I look!"

Rufus pursed his mouth and looked at me for confirmation, and I nodded back. In this mood nothing would stop Olympias, and something told me that this unexpected visit was not a break in the pattern of what we had just been saying.

The thin, dark man paused in the doorway for his eyes to grow accustomed to the dimmer light, then he walked quickly over to the bed.

Olympias fixed him with her penetrating eyes and started to speak without any of the polite formalities.

"Apollos, I didn't know I needed you till a moment ago, and now you're here!"

"I can see you aren't well. Is that how I can help you?"

If Olympias had been standing on her two feet she would have stamped one of them. "No, that isn't important except that it means I haven't the strength to explain things properly. Apollos, where will the next meeting be held?"

"At the house of Titus Justus as usual, in two days' time."

"The kalends, that's good, and the hour is still the same?"

"Yes, but Olympias. . . ."

"No, not for me, for Timandra and perhaps one other. The promise is coming into my hand. You see, child, there are some things it is better to see than to talk about, and I don't think you would be shy to go among strangers, and to go with your mind open to what you would see, even if it seemed nothing like the worship of any god you have heard about. Now, will you go outside for a moment?"

I went out puzzled and shaken by what I had heard, and at once their low and urgent voices started again.

Dion came quickly through into the garden courtyard, wriggled out of the heavy folds of his toga and flung it across a marble bench. He stood with his hands gripping his elbows tightly, trembling with some strong emotion. There was the same bleak look in his eyes I had seen before on the day he hurt his foot.

Then he saw me and came over quickly, but when I waited for him to speak he was silent.

"What is it?" I asked, knowing I was not making sense but saying the first thing that came into my head. "You haven't been to that place again, the workshop?"

"I may be stupid, Urbinus says I am, but not enough for that. No, Timandra, I don't think I can tell you; at least I can be clever enough not to hurt you with what hurt me. Yet as I was walking back it was you I wanted to talk to."

"Tell me if it would help."

"But I don't think it would make sense to anyone else, it's just that a lot of little things that have been happening have suddenly added up. It's been such a strange summer, Timandra, ever since Prisca died; before that I can't ever remember a time when so many things seemed suddenly different."

"It's not just that you're getting older?"

"You're probably right, and that's it, but it doesn't make it any easier for me to make sense out of my life. I may really be stupid—Timandra, it hurt when Urbinus said that, it was the look on his face—but it's been a happy sort of stupidness. Wouldn't it have been much better, much more beautiful, if the world really had been the simpler place I thought it was, when I read my books and only saw what I wanted to see?"

"Then you hurt your foot and couldn't run in the games, and that made you look at them and understand that something you had set your heart on wouldn't have been worth doing anyway?"

"Yes, that was the beginning of it for me. So I started to spend more time with my brother; I found I could actually be useful to him, carrying messages unobtrusively, and being there to be talked to. I thought I was beginning to understand the way people and affairs and rival interests fit together and govern a city like Corinth."

He looked across at me as we stood in the colonnade near the doorway of Olympias's room; with the brilliance of the light behind him I could not see his face clearly, only that he looked older in the way he had on the day of Vipsanius's trial, and that his eyes seemed tired. Then I understood what he was talking about, the thing he had tried not to tell me.

"It's something about Vipsanius, isn't it?" I asked.

His whole body jerked and he half turned away, still with his hands gripping his elbows as if he was cold in that burning heat, and I knew that it was the only way that he could keep from trembling.

"Yes," he said, his face still hidden. "You see I realized that I had taken the message to the proconsul's residence, that led to Vipsanius's arrest. Urbinus had betrayed him deliberately, no, not really betrayed because there was no plot, only a way of thinking and some future plans that could be dangerous for the stability of the city. We are so delicately poised between Rome and Greece."

"And from that one letter the proconsul acted, the man was tried, allowed to kill himself, and the next day his wife was found with her veins cut. The master may have been right, Dion, there may have been great danger."

"I don't know, perhaps his death will help the city, but I

can't stop feeling that a wrong thing like that can never lead to good, or not a good worth having."

"But you mind most because it was the master's decision, and he used you when you didn't know what you were doing, that's why it hurts so," I said, suddenly wise.

"I suppose so, Timandra. It feels as if another door has been slammed in my face. If that is the way my brother lives I don't see how I can be part of it, and I don't know where to go or what to think about."

Olympias's voice called me.

"I think I know what you should do," I said. "This summer seems like a maze, but your grandmother holds the thread that may guide us to the centre."

"And the minotaur will be there to welcome us!"

"No, I don't think so. There's somewhere she wants me to go—some people I'm to listen to. I don't understand anything about it yet, but if she says I should go, then I must. You feel now that your brother betrayed you as well as Vipsanius, but your grandmother could never betray either of us; if you are looking for something to believe in, believe in her. I think you may be meant to come to this meeting with me."

6 · TIMOTHEOS

I spent the next two days in a very strange state of mind, completely occupied in my work—for life in that household left no time for dreaming—and yet expectant. Not really of a new god, but of something beyond being a slave, some light behind a closed curtain, and that was enough to start with.

Olympias seemed suddenly her old self, with energy enough to organize the whole household. I think it would have been more complicated to arrange for Dion to be out of the house on an unexplained night errand than for me, but fortunately Urbinus was expected to be away and would not need to know. I could see that Nerea was not listening when Olympias told her about me, and Hegiso was more delighted at the chance to put the baby to bed than concerned about why.

Then as the shadows grew deeper on the appointed day and I went to find the thick veil I always wore when I went out, I was suddenly cold and frightened and wanted nothing so much as to stay at home. But the look of anticipation on Olympias's face when I went into her room was enough to keep me silent about my own feelings. We left by the side door just before sunset, a strange little group, Dion ahead, then myself two steps behind because I could not walk beside my master's brother in the street, and lastly Hermas the outdoor slave who would light us home when the streets were dark. The familiar road towards the market was crowded with people going home for the night, but it felt quite unfamiliar to me that evening.

It is an effort now to think back twelve years to remember what I saw and felt at that meeting. The words, most of them, have gone, and it is faces I remember. First seen in the light of the small courtyard outside the house next door to the synagogue and then in a room that seemed dark after the brilliant glow of the setting sun outside. Yet the lamps were already lit and the faces were clear enough, as if the light on them came partly from within.

We had heard them singing from across the courtyard though it did not seem that we were late, only that those who were early had started as soon as they arrived. There were perhaps thirty people there and that made the room seem full; some were sitting on stools and benches around those who were plainly the leaders, some stood against the walls and there were children in front on the floor. I knew no one except Apollos, who sat between Titus, the merchant who owned the house, and a dark young man.

Apollos saw us in the doorway as the old porter led us in; he got up quickly to take our hands and lead us to one of the benches. The people moved up for us and it did not seem strange there that Dion should be sitting beside me or that he should take my hand and hold it tight, as if we were awed children on our first day at a new school.

The singing was still going on. For a little while I was too shy even to raise my head, it was when I did that I first saw the faces.

I had never before seen so many people looking happy. Even at a family feast there are some who are drunk or bad-tempered. These people were of one mind and it was a happy one. There was a middle-aged lady who must by her dress be the wife of a councillor, a soldier from the garrison in uniform, and a young lad with a bruised face and a split lip; he was singing with the rest, men and women like any you pass in the street.

Everyone but us seemed to know the words and the tune was simple and often repeated, with a deep surging note. When it was finished the young man beside Apollos began another. Dion's hand tightened in mine.

"The heavens tell the glory of God, the sky proclaims his work, day speaks to day," Dion sang with the others; Apollos saw him and smiled. I began to hum the tune very softly.

I had known that I would not find a temple, but I had expected that the room where Olympias's friends met would at least show some signs that a god was worshipped there. But there were no hangings, no shrine or statue even like the ones I saw every day in the atrium of the villa Torquartii; only dining-room couches pushed back and the last crumbs of a meal on the floor that there had not been time to clear away because the guests had come early.

Then the singing stopped and Titus stood up. "Brothers, it's good that we can be free to meet together to praise the Lord, and joy to me that it is in my own house. Still, some of you must be away from here before the city gates close at the eleventh hour, so we must stop singing for the moment. Apollos, will you lead us in prayer?"

The faces were graver now. Most of the men stood up and some raised their hands. The councillor's wife who was sitting in front of me remained with her head bowed; we did not move, trying not to be noticed.

"Loving Father, maker of everything in heaven and earth, Father of our beloved Lord," prayed Apollos, his face lifted and illuminated as if he spoke to someone he could see through his closed eyelids. "We praise you for your goodness in bringing us together tonight, that you who have created the stars and seas, all powerful, should have opened the gates that could have shut us from each other, that you have softened the hearts of those who would have kept us apart from our brothers and sisters. Now, even as we begin to worship you together, give us peace in our hearts that you will smooth our way home, and that we may be certain that when we leave each other we cannot leave you. Dear Father, we pray for those we have left at home who do not know you, who are still bound in misery by their sin. You know them, they are even dearer to you than they are to us; we pray that with your power we may become the means by which you can bless each one of them."

The prayer was a long one, and as Apollos moved from one theme to another, confession of sin, thanksgiving for blessing, and then a great cry for the needs of others, murmurs of agreement ran across the hall like wind ripples on still water. It was not the prayer, the formula of correct words that a priest says before an altar on behalf of men who have handed responsibility for their worship to him. This was the praying of all put into the voice of one.

But whom were they praying to? This God did not seem to have a name, except that he was a father, and that one of his sons was specially beloved because of some great suffering that he had undergone. I thought of Mithras and Adonis, Osiris, and all the other young gods I had ever heard of who had suffered and died, but this seemed to be none of them. Then I understood that Olympias had not sent us to be taught about a new god but to see how people behaved when they believed in him. I had cried to her out of my fear at the darkness before me; had these people the secret of a light that did not fail?

I felt quieter then, not trying to understand what was happening, only to see and listen and feel. As the minutes passed the woman sitting in front with bowed head began to tremble; I began to watch her and it came into my mind that she was going to faint, so I edged forward on the bench to be ready to catch her if she did, for no one else seemed to have noticed her distress.

Then Apollos stopped and she stood up quickly. "Brothers and sisters, before God I must tell you that I have failed in my following of the Way of our Lord."

She paused, for her voice had broken, and the men and women turned to her with grave and attentive faces. But what can she have done that they or their God could think so wrong, I wondered? Anyone can see even at a first glance that she is a good woman, and I wish I had her for my mistress and not a sick and unbalanced girl.

"Chloe, tell us what the Lord has laid on your heart," said Apollos quietly.

"How can we be so blind when Our Lord shows us the way so very clearly?" she asked, in a soft voice that still shook with pain. "All this time, ever since my baptism, there has been a part of my life that I have shut away. It's as if I had come to my husband when we were married and said, 'This house has been mine and now I am giving it all to you, because I love you, only not this room, I have kept the key to the door and I shall not unlock it for you.' My Lord has taught me that all men and women living are one family, and that I may not hate any one of my brothers and sisters. Yet you remember three years ago, in my great trouble, when my husband died; there were people then who were unkind to me, my husband's brother and his wife. In my bitterness then I said that I would never speak to them again, and in all this time I have not, although now the woman is ill. And I never saw until tonight that in this I was shutting the Lord out of a part of my life. How can he use me for his work if I am not clean for his light to shine through? When there is this smear of hate across me?" She put her hands up to her face and began to cry quietly.

"Brothers and sisters," Apollos's clear, grave voice cut

through the murmur of sympathy and love. "Through our
sister our Lord has a lesson for all of us. There are some of us
here who have done things that even the men of this city
would call evil—murders, acts of cruelty and injustice, we
shudder to think of them even now. And the Lord washed the
stain of them away and broke the power they had to cripple
our lives and made us new men. But there are other things
which we know to be sins because they bring misery and
divide us from our Lord, even though most men and women
think that they are the way all humans behave. The tempta-
tion to them is with us every hour of our lives, as Chloe has
shown us. While we pray for our sister we should all search
our own hearts for the one face that our Lord may show us,
the one man about whom we have thought 'Surely the Lord
did not really mean me to love even you'. Now, Chloe, do
you know what you must do?"

She took her hands away from her face and sat down
wearily on the bench; the plump young servant girl who had
been sitting beside her put an arm round her. Then she
looked up at the tall man and she was smiling, although her
face was still wet with tears.

"Yes, I know, and truly our God is powerful, for it is something I could not possibly do by myself. Will you pray for me
that even now I may not falter, as I go to that family in for-
giveness and love?"

"Titus, will you come with me?" asked Apollos.

Stools were moved so that the two men could come to the
seated woman. The young servant would have moved too,
but her mistress held her fast by the hand. Then the ministers
laid their hands on her bent head, with low words of prayer,
and there was peace and a very great stillness so that I gripped
Dion's hand hard enough to have hurt him if he had not been
gripping me back, for hands had become precious things, the
servants of blessing.

Then as the men drew back and looked down at her Chloe began to sing, without any words that I could understand, soft and high, and other voices joined hers, weaving across the melody till there was a web of sound that was like the light thrown upwards from a lamp or the triumph of the sun when it is half-hidden by stormclouds, more than a human song. I saw tears shine on other faces raised around the room and felt my own cheeks wet, partly through the beauty of the singing, and partly because they knew why they sang and I did not.

When the voices had fallen silent the prayers began again, a few words at a time from many voices. It was like a family gathered round a father they have not seen for a time, children's short incoherent messages, the elders more thoughtful and considered. I was tired now and stopped listening to all that was said, even when Apollos stood up to teach. What he said was like a story to someone who begins to listen just before the end; without the beginning it did not make much sense. I heard him as I had heard the waves on the rocks of Samos as a child, and in their measure and their thunder there was the same deep, healing peace. I remembered Olympias then, lying alone in pain, with the two of us held in her mind by a love that had wanted this hour for us and had willed us to be here as if it was the most precious gift that she could give. Even now her thought would still be on us. My memory of the last months taught me then my first lesson in prayer, of the faith and need that a God worthy of Olympias must answer.

It was dark outside now and the lamps that had burned pale at first in the light from the high windows made warm pools that lit the intent faces and cast the shadow of Apollos far across the walls. Tired as I was I knew that the evening was nearly over and I did not want it to end, however little I had understood of what had happened. Beyond this pale lamplight the darkness would be black indeed.

They sang again, standing with arms raised. Dion pulled

me to my feet and we stood with them, caught up in an emotion that made us dumb while in their freedom the men and women around us sang even more joyfully. Yes, I thought, peace and freedom. I don't know where it comes from, but I have seen it now with my own eyes, and what other light can a slave use to guide her steps?

When the hymn was finished the lady Chloe turned and saw us for the first time. She stood puzzled with her head on one side, then she stretched out her hands to Dion.

"Olympias! You are the grandson. I can't have seen you since you were a child, but you have her eyes!"

I wondered that I had not noticed it for myself before, but she was right, of course, and it explained a good deal. Now that I could see Chloe's face I wished even more that she was my mistress, for it was generous and calm. I smiled shyly at the slave-girl, while Dion answered loving inquiries about himself and the health of Olympias.

"She has been failing this summer, we can all see it. Will you come to see her, madam? You must be old friends and I'm sure it would give her pleasure."

A shadow crossed Chloe's face. "It's stupid that I haven't been for so long. There was difficulty some years back between the men of our families, and at one time my husband forbade me. Now he is dead I have no excuse for my forgetfulness. I'll try to come tomorrow."

I was glad at the thought of this gentle woman in the often troubled house of Urbinus, and I smiled. She turned to me then, and I bobbed a little curtsy, expecting, even there in the house of Titus, the always patronizing interest of a matron in even the most promising slave, but she only asked me my name.

"Timandra," she repeated it after me. "Metella, we will remember that, won't we?"

Her slave nodded and touched my hand in farewell.

The room was nearly empty by then, but before we could go Apollos came to us with the young man who had sat beside him all the evening.

"I know," he said, looking down at Dion with a warm understanding. "It's late and you're tired, and you have heard either too much or too little! But before you go here is Timotheos, whom you should talk to. He will be able to answer your questions better than I can. Now, Timandra."

He drew me to one side. "I was grieved by the change in Olympias when I saw her two days ago. How is she now?"

"Better than for a month tonight, almost too strong, I think."

"Yes, she will have been very happy these last two days."

His words made me shiver, though I did not know why.

"Do you understand? I can see that in the few months you have been in the house she has come to love and put much trust in you."

"Yes, I think so. She is trying to do something for Dion, and for me too. I know already what her kindness has meant to me; I can't explain properly, it's not that I've been ill-treated, but that without her a part of me would have died."

"She has lived according to our Way for nearly five years now. Her dearest wish was to bring Dion to us, but she knew it must be in the Lord's time not hers, and she saw the time growing very short. Will you try to get word to me if she should seem worse in the next few days? I leave for Ephesus again at the full moon."

The two young men were talking together when Apollos left me, and I watched them, weary and wanting to be back with Olympias. Timotheos was not much over twenty, and as Greek to look at as Dion, or so I thought till I noticed his dark eyes.

"So we're both half one thing and half another," he said, laughing, obviously liking Dion as much as I had when I first saw him. "Only my mother was Jewish; I come from Galatia. Can I talk to you, Dion? Not tonight when you're tired. I work in the mornings for one of the brothers who is a potter—I'm lodging at his house—but from about the seventh hour I'm free. Ask for me at the Street of the Tilemakers. His name is Drusus."

"I'll come," said Dion. "Yes, really I will. I must talk to someone, there's so much . . . you understand?"

"I do indeed. I was about your age too, when I first heard, or saw actually. I'd gone for a walk one afternoon and I saw one man heal another who was a cripple; or that was how it looked. There was a riot, but I knew I had to know more about the man who could use a power like that. Can I say one thing for tonight, though? I don't know what you are thinking about what you've heard and seen, though your face shows me something. You may have felt the first tugging of a power that can be overwhelming, but with it, it brings danger. No, two dangers."

"Your faith isn't proscribed?"

"No, not yet anyway, but I wasn't thinking of civil power—danger from a guard hammering on your door at midnight! This is something more subtle. As the power of our God works in us, another power will try to work against him. No enemy likes to see his outposts overrun, and we know that this world is a battlefield. Our enemy has clever weapons. He may say on the way home, in your heart, 'Now that was all very trivial, slaves and silly women in a room singing songs. Remember the great annual festival of Poseidon—now there is a God and a way of worship'."

Dion laughed, "I see, now what is the other danger?"

"Trouble. The unexpected waiting for you at home, or tomorrow in the city. The stone that turns under your sandal to break your ankle and make you quite absorbed by your body for days and days, till the memory of tonight has faded.

Something like that, I don't know what, but it's an attack most of us have known, sooner or later. You look as if you don't believe me, but we'll see if I'm right."

I knew he was, and I spoke before I remembered my place. "Dion, things do happen like that. Remember when you split your toenail?"

He swung round and for a moment I thought he was angry with me; then he smiled. "Timotheos, this is Timandra, my sister-in-law's maid, she seems to understand you even if I don't. I can't explain now what she's talking about, for it was a painful day in more ways than one, but it had its good side for it gave me her for a friend."

The colour rose in my face at words that made my heart very full, but I looked Timotheos in the eye for all that as he greeted me, and I was glad when he smiled that I was already blushing for another reason. There was that in his dark Jewish eyes in the Greek face that for the first time since I came to Chenchraea might have put the bitter fear of men out of my heart.

"Sister, you are all Greek, I can see," he said. "And from your voice you're an islander. You haven't been a slave long?"

"Four months, sir. When Dion comes to you, speak to him for both of us. I shall be busy at home and I don't know when I shall be free to come again."

"My name is Timotheos," he said. "And I shall surely remember you in messages and answers."

Hermas was half-asleep in the outer courtyard, the only slave left. Yawning as if he would split, he lit his torch from a lamp and went ahead out into the dark streets.

"Keep close," said Dion. "It's later than I thought. Here, take my arm."

I hung on gratefully, for it was very dark in spite of the jumping torch light, and the paving stones were worn and uneven. From the shadows of a doorway a beggar woke and stretched out a stick-thin arm, and a tethered dog barked viciously. As we turned into the Laechium road the light was a little better, for here there were a few torches stuck into holders in the walls. Some way ahead three drunken men broke suddenly from a lighted doorway. Dion stopped short, holding me closer, but they turned off by a side alley before they saw us. The noises of a hot night in the city sounded different heard from outside the safety of our high walls. A cart clattered by, come in late from the harbour before the gates closed; a horseman nearly rode us down from behind, coming from the direction of the proconsul's house. Once a woman laughed just above us, behind a lighted window, a short shrill sound.

As we turned the last corner and the house was almost in sight, I loosened my tight grip on Dion's arm. Then he laughed under his breath.

"It was rather ridiculous, when you think of it. A well-dressed matron confessing that she's quarrelled with her sister-in-law!"

"That's just what Timotheos said you'd think." The thought of it made me breathless, and I spoke quickly, there would not be much more time. "Don't you see, for me that's terribly important. We don't know anything really about what these people believe, but small things, like how people treat their families, can mean as much as big. Your grandmother has held on to something all these years that has made her bedroom the only peaceful place in the house. That's power. So is something that can prevent you from hating anyone, master or slave. That could be more wonderful than the power to split Acrocorinth with lightning. It would work differently, but it would be just as miraculous."

"Like leaven."

"Just that. But Dion, we must remember the second warning!"

7 · TROUBLE

We went down the lane at the side of the house and in through the garden door. Dion had the key. Even there in the dark shadow of the fruit trees, away from the main part of the house, I knew at once that something was wrong. There were too many lights, and I could hear Hegiso's raised voice.

"Olympias!" I whispered.

Nerea got up from a stool by the high bed, as I came quickly into the old woman's room, dropping my veil on the chest by the door. The small room was untidy, with a stained cover kicked out of the way and a bowl of water still standing on the floor. Rhodippe was huddled in the corner crying and Nerea's face was tearstained and desperate.

"Timandra, where have you been? I couldn't remember. Oh, it doesn't matter. Look, poor Grandmother, how can she have done it? We heard a cry and ran, and there she was on the floor."

From the other side of the bed I looked down on the fleshless face of a stranger, not the much loved Olympias of the last months. Her wrinkled skin had shrunk as close to the gaunt bones of brow and nose and chin as a thin rain-soaked tunic sticks to the body; her mouth was a small dark hole in her face, and clotted blood and bruising spread across her brow.

I picked up one limp, brown-mottled wrist. The bones

moved under the skin like thin sticks loosely wrapped in cloth, and the pulse flickered and trembled, hardly there at all.

Dion had come in behind me; he went to Nerea and put his arms round her, and she began to cry noisily, like a little girl. I knew then that our problem would be with her, not Olympias, during the last short hours that she would be with us. And the master was not home yet.

Dion shook Nerea gently. "Have you sent for Urbinus?"

"There hasn't been time."

He looked at me over her head. "It's very late now and he was at the house of Junius Piso on the other side of the city. A messenger might miss him. Nerea, it must have been terrible finding her like that, you should lie down till he comes."

She raised her face from his shoulder and looked at me piteously. "Oh, Timandra, will she . . . will she soon . . . ?"

"My lady, I don't think she can live more than a few hours, perhaps not so long. After that blow she might be witless."

Dion drew in his breath through his teeth; Olympias mindless and wandering was not to be thought about. But I did not think it would come to that, not with the shock and a blow on the head, and perhaps other injuries I had not seen.

Nerea had stopped crying, she stood looking lost and uncomprehending till Hegiso surged into the room.

"Come, my little love, let Hegiso bathe your face. Come with me now."

Nerea allowed herself to be led away like a child, and Rhodippe followed them.

"Now," I said.

I bent close over Olympias and turned her head gently on the pillow, then I pulled the cover back. It was clear how she had fallen, over on to her head and left shoulder; but what could have made her raise herself so far in the bed that this was possible? I had not known her arms were strong enough.

TROUBLE

There was nothing any of us who loved her could do now but be with her during the last hours when her spirit fluttered to loose itself from her body.

Dion moved away from the bed as I straightened the cover and began to tidy the room automatically. He let the toga slip slowly off his left shoulder and then, as its weight pulled at his arm, he folded it up mechanically and put it down. The years slid from him with it and turned him from the thoughtful young man who had comforted Nerea to a miserable boy.

"Must she die?" he asked.

"Would you keep her, like this?" I smoothed the hair back gently from the bruised face.

"Timotheos said trouble might come, but could his God let evil be loosed so cruelly on our grandmother, just because we went to the meeting tonight? Would a just God do that?"

"I don't know about justice, but it might be something to do with love, and what people will pay for love. Do you want a god to heal her for you, then?"

"I don't know what I want. Wait, though. Her voice, Timandra. I think I shall miss that most. If she once opened her eyes and asked about the meeting, and we could tell her..."

"Yes, to tell her it was ... I don't know, good doesn't seem to be the word; and to say goodbye."

"A god could do that?"

"Yes, the God Apollos prayed to, could."

"Should we send to him? He asked us to let him know if she was worse."

"I don't think there's time. She looks like my father did during the last night. She can't live long, hardly till morning. But she believed. No, it wouldn't be right to pray that if a god let Olympias speak again we'd believe in him. If it's right in itself it will happen."

Dion came and stood so close to me at the end of the bed

that I could feel that he was trembling. He bowed his head.

"Timandra, I'm scared and I . . . can't. I don't think I could say the words. Pray for both of us. Now, so it can be before anyone comes."

I opened my mouth and no sound came. Then I was trembling too, and cold, like a child trying to find the voice for a difficult confession. Only I was asking and one cannot ask someone who is not there.

"God whom Olympias loved, give her back to us for a minute . . if it won't hurt her too much. Please, we don't understand, but she did."

Dion gasped as if he had been holding his breath and then let it out with a rush. He sat down on the side of the bed and took one of the tiny twisted hands between his long brown fingers. It was so quiet in the room I could hear my own breathing.

The dark circle of Olympias's mouth closed as firmly as a touched sea anemone. I dropped down on my knees on the stool by the bed so that my face was level with hers.

The voice came before she opened her eyes, a thread of sound, but as dry and decisive as Olympias's had always been.

"Let the words of my mouth and the thoughts of my heart
Be acceptable in your sight, My God, my rock, and my saviour."

Dion bent close. "Where does it say that, Grandmother?"
The withered eyelids flickered. "You know, in the scroll. Dion?"
"Yes?"
"You're back then. I thought you'd gone to Titus's house and I was waiting, and then I saw . . . no, never mind."
"Dear Grandmother, it was all you promised." I took her other hand.
Then just for a moment she opened her eyes and looked at both of us. "And I was right, and He is very good."

TROUBLE

Her eyes closed and her head turned slightly on the pillow. We neither of us moved for a while, deep in a mystery that was completely beyond understanding. It was only the distant sounds of Urbinus's arrival that brought us to ourselves. Dion laid Olympias's hand back on the covers and turned to me; his face was wet with tears.

Urbinus, with Rufus behind him, came quickly into the room. It seemed suddenly full and airless, with their large shadows jumping back from the small lamps by the bed, and their helplessness at this sudden distress.

"Oh, not like this," whispered Urbinus, his normally decided voice broken. "Not in pain and so quickly!"

"I don't think there was much pain, my lord," I said gently. "The blood and the bruising make it look worse. She must have fainted as soon as she was hurt, until just now."

"She spoke to you?" He swung round to Dion.

"Yes, just a few words and then she seemed to go to sleep. She was very much at peace."

"What did she say?"

Dion hesitated. Had what she had said been only for us? But Urbinus was also her grandson, we had no right to keep silent. "It was some words from the Jewish writings she loved so much." He repeated them.

"They were a prayer to a god?"

"She believed so."

Urbinus did not understand. He stood for a moment, then brushed the idea away. "Timandra, you've seen this before. She can't live?"

"Not many hours, but no one can tell how long. I don't think there is anything to be done except to stay with her in case she should come to herself again. But, sir, the mistress is very distressed, it was she who found her."

"Yes, of course, I'll go to her." He looked at our tired faces. "Some of us should get what rest we can. Dion, go to bed now, we'll wake you after midnight, if there's any need. Timandra, will you watch for the moment, until I come back?"

He went out with Dion, but Rufus stayed behind, large and strangely comforting. I sat down on the stool by the head of the bed where I could hold Olympias's hand, though I was certain she would not regain consciousness again. Rufus leant back against the wall on the other side of the room.

After a long silence he said unexpectedly, "This house will be like an unlit lamp without her. There's stormy water ahead."

"But Nerea is stronger now!"

"For how long? She depended on Olympias."

"She has a good husband."

"Yes, indeed, or we should have done much worse before now. But he has his duties, he has no time to spare for a wife's fancies. If he ever stopped to see what is underneath his nose would he trouble to understand a woman who will not even cross her own doorstep?"

"That's hard!"

He had been speaking to the floor, arms crossed, heavy brows frowning. Now he looked up and his dark eyes were shrewd above the twisted cheek and mouth. "Not hard, true. Nerea is ailing, but she needs a priest, not a doctor. Prisca told me something and I've noticed more for myself. Our mistress needs the help of a stronger god than any I've heard tell of."

"Olympias's God?"

"The Jewish prophet? What does he care about a Roman Greek?"

"But he created everyone, didn't he? I don't know, I don't understand yet."

"I would believe in any god who turned Nerea into a normal woman."

Then we were both quiet with our own thoughts, waiting.

From time to time Olympias's breathing changed to a long snoring sound, and then what seemed like silence, so that I bent forward, watchful. But the pulse flickered on, under my fingers.

The house beyond the room grew quiet, and the night beyond in the city. It was after midnight, and the wind was blowing in short dry gusts down from the gulf that rustled the fig leaves in the courtyard. I was nearly asleep but part of my mind was loose and clear, and able to plan. Rufus had been right about the stormy water ahead. We would be coming back to the old difficult times just after Pyrrha was born. But then there had been nothing I could do, now I knew the household, and around me was the warmth of a new hope, not certain, not to be fully understood, but of more than one tree for Nerea to cling to for strength, a whole forest. In that room, watching over a dying woman, I first looked at the unbounded possibility of God, not as one among many, but as one alone. One who could give words back to a woman on the threshold of death, could comfort a girl whose spirit was still wounded from the cruelty she had seen as a child.

Rufus stirred and stretched. There were footsteps outside and Urbinus came in, crumpled and unshaven in his limp party undertunic. He stood looking down from the end of the bed.

"No change? Nerea is asleep now. Hegiso gave her a poppy drink. Timandra, go and rest while you can. There will be the baby and your mistress for you to care for after tonight is over. I'll wake Dion before dawn."

I got up unwillingly and laid the twisted hand down on the covers, then I went quickly out of the room before the tears had time to come, because I knew he was right, and I should be fit for nothing if I watched all night. Already it seemed an age since we had sung in the room in Titus's house, and Timotheos had asked Dion to come to the Street of the Tilemakers. And he must still go, now more than ever. I was sure of that as I took off my tunic in the airless darkness of my small room, with Pyrrha asleep in her cradle. A small lamp still burned behind the curtains in Nerea's room, and I could hear Hegiso snoring.

At first I did not think that I should sleep, even now when my tired body was at rest, but it came like the dark waves o the sea at night, to wash the hurt and fear from my mind.

There was light in the room when I woke. It must be after dawn and yet no one had come for me, although there was the sound of movement in the next room, and Pyrrha was waking and would soon be crying for her breakfast.

I felt more tired as I went to pick her up than I had when I went to sleep but I knew the feeling would pass. I picked the baby up and took her into her mother.

Nerea was sitting up in bed, flushed and heavy-eyed, with her thick, dark hair falling round her shoulders above the thin shift.

"Oh, my lamb!" she said, stretching out her arms for Pyrrha, and I understood how she felt, for there was great comfort in the feel of the warm baby with her urgent but easy needs.

Nerea settled Pyrrha to her breast and then looked up. "Go quickly, Timandra, and see. They would have come, wouldn't they, if it was the end? Oh, poor Grandmother . . ."

She started to cry into the baby's soft hair. Pyrrha lost the nipple, hiccuped and complained.

"Hush," I said, "you'll stop your milk."

I twisted my hair out of sight under a scarf and went quickly through the fresh, early morning light and shadow of the courtyard to the other doorway. The curtain had been drawn back but it still seemed strangely dark with the smoky lamps burning, here on the shadowed side of the garden. Dion and Urbinus were both bending over the bed, and at once I heard the change that the hours had brought. The deep rattling breaths shook the tiny body on the bed, and Olympias's eyes were half-open, but she was far, far beyond us now.

"No, it can't be long," said Urbinus, looking up when I came in and seeing my face. "How is my wife?"

"She was asking for news."

"I'll go to her for a moment now you're here. You'll call me?"

I stood beside Dion and he took my hand. Outside in the courtyard the light faded as a cloud covered the sun. The household was awake and a cart clattered by, the noise loud through the house wall that backed on to a lane. For a moment I lost the sound of the difficult breathing and bent down. The cart had passed and there was a new silence; I took up Olympias's wrist and the fluttering bird had flown.

"She's gone," I whispered, and then the sun came out again in the courtyard and there was peace around us in the room. Dion turned to me and briefly we clung together like two unhappy children and there were tears on both our faces, though neither of us knew that we were crying.

Then Dion drew away. "Urbinus!" he said, and went out, almost running.

I bent to kiss Olympias's bruised forehead, and tuck her hand under the covers. Then there was a cry across the courtyard, and hurrying feet. Urbinus came in, his face twisted with pain, and went down on his knees by the quiet bed.

"Why then, why just then?"

"There was no change, my lord. She breathed again and then she didn't. It could have been another hour," I said.

He did not look up. "Go to your mistress."

The other house slaves were gathering outside the doorway of Nerea's room, for she was hysterical and the baby, too, was screaming with shock and anger. I pushed through, took her from Hegiso and gave her to Rhodippe, who was nearest the doorway.

"Take her somewhere quiet and calm her down," I said firmly. "She'll have taken enough to last for the moment. And it looks as if she must be weaned in a hurry unless we can find a wet-nurse, so think about that—and goat's milk—while you're about it!" I pushed her out into the courtyard and Pyrrha's wails faded into the distance.

Nerea was throwing herself about on the bed and Dion was trying to control her. I bent across and slapped her firmly but not hard across the face, and then as she was shocked still for a moment took her in my arms.

"Hush then, you wouldn't have had her live on in pain, would you? She's peaceful now, and quiet, and with her God."

Hegiso still stood there, red-faced and malevolent, ready to make confusion rather than calm it.

"The master wants you," I said, over Nerea's bent head. She could do no harm there, though I would have been glad to prepare Olympias's body myself. Hegiso snorted and went out.

Nerea said into my shoulder, "Timandra, what will happen now? I'm so frightened."

As I stroked her hair and spoke to her I was looking at Dion over her bent head. "There's no need to be frightened, death isn't dangerous. This time it was merciful. Of course we must weep because we loved your grandmother and we shall miss her, but she believed she was going to a God who loved her. She was happy, when she spoke last night before she died. You must believe that."

"But I can't." It was a long wail of pain. "I don't know her God, and how could he let her hurt herself? Her face, Timandra, and the blood! Oh no, let her come back, let her come back."

Dion looked white and exhausted. This would be the first time for him, I remembered, since he was old enough to understand a death that was close to him. And as I had seen so quickly the night before, the problem was not now with Olympias dying but with Nerea living.

"We must get word to Apollos," I said to him, "and more than ever now you must talk to Timotheos. I can't leave my mistress."

"I can't go now, not with Grandmother lying dead. Secundus will have to be told and there's the funeral."

"Because of all this you must go." I had never been more certain of anything in my life. "If Timotheos had been a doctor to heal a sick body you would have gone at any hour. There's sickness here as great as any Olympias suffered from. I don't know how he can help, but I know he can; perhaps his God has told me so. Will you believe me? If there's an answer, something to be done, Timotheos knows what it is. Will you go?"

He stood up, looking at me with the eyes of someone who can be helped across a narrow place only by what he sees in the face of someone he can trust.

"I'm frightened, too, but I can see you aren't, and that matters a lot. If Timotheos can tell me why, I'll go to him this afternoon, when I can. Will that satisfy you?"

"I hope I'm right," I thought. "God of Olympias, let me be right."

8 · CHLOE

Olympias was to be buried the day after she had died, in the family tomb beside the road from Corinth to Laechium. As that first difficult morning passed the house became quieter; Secundus had been sent for, and I liked him better standing quite at a loss for words beside the tidy body on Olympias's bed, than I had ever thought would be possible. Little though he had considered her in recent years, he must have loved her when he was a child. After the first arrangements had been made Urbinus spent the main part of the day in the atrium, sitting in front of the family shrine, receiving the close members of the clan who came with the usual words and offerings, and the clients and hangers-on who were afraid to miss any event at the house of a magistrate.

I could not leave Nerea all day, but when she was lying half-asleep in the worst of the midday heat Dion slipped into the room with a bulge in the fold of his tunic.

"I have the scrolls from Grandmother's room," he said quietly. "Hegiso is already sorting her things away, and I was afraid they would be lost. I suppose I must give them back to Apollos."

"Oh no, must you?"

"I'll take them to Titus's house anyway and ask him. I know how you feel; she left nothing else that was half so precious. Then I'll go to the Street of the Tilemakers. Can we talk after dinner? There'll be a lot to tell you."

"On the summer terrace if I can get away."

What Dion had said consoled me for the long difficult afternoon, with Nerea alternately tearful and sunk in despair. I kept remembering the two young men and envying them their freedom to meet and talk. Then Chloe came.

Rufus preceded her from the atrium, which Urbinus had only just left, to rest after the last of the callers.

"There's this lady," he said. "She asked for Domina Olympias, and when I told her what had happened she wanted to speak to you. How does she know your name? She's Domina Chloe Aemilia, and it's years since one of her family was here."

"Where is she? I'll come at once."

"Just out there in the garden. She's a forceful lady."

Chloe was sitting on one of the marble benches on the shady side of the courtyard, with the servant Metella standing behind her holding a large fan. It had been hot in Nerea's stuffy room, but outside the scorching air seemed to press on the body like a solid weight. I knew I must be looking draggled and weary as I crossed quickly to the welcome shade.

The lady took my hands in hers, as if I had been an old friend. "Oh, Timandra, all these years when my family's pride kept me away, and now I'm one day too late! Did she die at peace?"

I told her what had happened, and of Olympias's last words.

"The Lord is good," she whispered. "He answered her, at the end. Apollos told me there was hardly a waking hour in the years since she knew our God, when she did not pray that those of her household might have the same blessing, and for Him to send someone, a sister or brother, to be with her. After that her thought was always for Dion, and when I saw him last night I understood why. Where the Lord has given so much he will ask a great deal, and it won't be easy. Still, he has you, as she did."

"But I'm not a believer. I don't even know who it is I should believe in, only that you and Domina Olympias understand a power that is stronger than anything I've ever believed in, stronger than Isis or Poseidon who let my father's ship be rammed. And there's something in your power that draws me towards you. I wish it could touch my mistress."

"She is in very great distress?"

"It isn't a normal sorrow. Already she's given herself a fever, and tomorrow with the funeral will be even worse."

"Yes, I know what an ordeal that can be when one is so deeply grieved."

"No, I didn't mean she would go with the mourners, she hasn't left the house since she was married." I explained then what Olympias had told me of the deep hurt that still scarred Nerea's mind.

"And this has been allowed to go on all these years, like an injury bandaged but not healed? Her mother must have been mad, and her husband. Metella, this is a real work of the evil one."

"Yes, my lady, I was thinking the same. What can we do?"

"I'm not sure. I must think."

She got up and walked slowly to the corner where honeysuckle had been trained up the pillars to the roof of the arcade. I could smell the flowers even from where I stood. Metella drew me down on the seat beside her, now that her mistress had gone.

"I don't understand. What is she doing?" I asked the older girl.

She smiled at me. "Asking for guidance. My mistress has been given a grace from the Lord to understand the hurts that people have suffered in their minds and bodies. It may be that she will be shown what should be done to heal Domina Nerea."

"But how could that possibly happen?"

"Only by God, not us, but in many ways—if we have the faith to believe that it is possible. It can be no part of His will for a woman to have been bound by such an evil for so long." She put an arm round me, for we were sitting close enough for her to feel me tremble. "No, don't be frightened, this isn't some terrifying magic to make anyone afraid, only the love a father has flowing through us to his other children. Now, do you think your mistress will let us see her?"

I smiled. "I shan't even ask her. Oh, Metella, can your God really do this, now, at once?"

"Perhaps, but this hurt is very deep, it may be a long time before Domina Nerea fully understands the freedom that is so near for her to take."

Chloe came back to us with her face grave. I signed for them both to wait in the doorway and went ahead into Nerea's room. She was lying on her back with her eyes closed and even the thin cover kicked back. She looked very young, with her hair loose, and the small air of authority that had come during the last months all wept away. When I had tidied her I beckoned them in.

Chloe's face was full of pity. "Nerea, do you remember me? I knew your mother, and when you were little I brought my daughter to play with you. Do you remember Lucilla?"

Nerea's eyes opened stickily. The name she knew but this woman's face was unfamiliar. "Lucilla? That was a long time ago, before . . . no, I don't remember when."

"And I knew the grandmother who has just gone from you. My dear, it's a great grief for you. She was the wisest woman I ever knew. You were fortunate to marry into such a family."

"I know," Nerea wailed. "And now she's gone I can't bear it. I don't know what to do without her." She sat up, her eyes wild.

Chloe went straight to the bed and took her hands. "These griefs come because death has to come, but it's not the death itself that is terrible, through it we go to God, it's when there is cruelty and unkindness with it. These we can fight. Olympias was wise and full of years, and she was ready for her death, she went content. If you knew, really knew, that she was in great joy now, would you call her back to that twisted body?"

"But how can I know?"

It seemed as if Chloe was changing the subject. "Did you trust your mother when you were a little girl; and your nurse?" She looked up at me for the name.

"Prisca," I whispered.

"Yes, Prisca, I remember her, a kind soul, and she loved you very much."

"Ye—es, of course I trusted them. They loved me."

"Then you know how it is possible to trust, because you know why. Will you trust me?" Nerea raised her tear-swollen eyes to the face of the older woman. It was a face no longer young, but one that I had trusted myself the moment I saw it.

Nerea did not say anything. She still sat up with her feet curled under her like a child, holding Chloe's hands, and quieter than she had been all day. All at once she slid forward and buried her head in Chloe's breast. The woman drew her close, stroking her hair, while above the bent head her lips were moving soundlessly and her eyes were closed. I saw that Metella behind her was also praying.

There was peace so that I could feel it, like a sudden smell of the sea, or of cornfields after spring rain. Nerea gave a little sigh and sat up.

"You are kind to come to me when it's so many years since I saw you. And you haven't seen my baby yet. Timandra?"

Pyrrha was waking up in her cradle under the fruit trees, with Hegiso asleep beside her on a stool. I brought her in to her mother, to be admired and loved, and smile wet, enchanting smiles at the strangers.

"She'll be such a comfort to me now," said Nerea, suddenly sad again, but still with this unfamiliar calm, holding the baby close. "Although Grandmother could not leave her room the whole house feels empty already—and yet she's still lying there." I thought she was going to cry again, but she only dropped her face to kiss the damp hair on Pyrrha's forehead.

"May I see her to say goodbye, after all these years? Your farewells will be at the family tomb tomorrow, but that isn't a time for strangers."

"Oh no, that will be for the men, my husband . . . I couldn't go."

"It's very hard, isn't it," said Chloe quietly, "to follow one much loved on a last journey? My Lucilla died, you know, three years ago. I lay awake all the last night, knowing I had not got the strength to do it. But it was given to me, and I went her last journey with her, as I had brought her to her first."

"How?"

"You know already, for you have a child. I loved her more than I loved my grief for her. Nerea, may I come again, when the mourning is over?"

As I took her to the room where the empty body of Olympias lay, I still did not know what had been done, or who had done it, but there had been a change and one beyond any normal power.

Nerea was very quiet for the rest of the afternoon, but she got up and dressed ready to eat with her husband and his brothers. Rufus saw her coming into the dining-room only just in time to lay the extra place. Dion was almost late, he hurried in quickly behind the others, still breathless. The meal was soon over and Nerea went straight to bed. I slipped out of the room as soon as she was settled, knowing that Dion would be waiting for me, but Urbinus was standing under the honeysuckle, deep in thought. He called my name as I passed him.

"Domina Nerea has asked me to order the litter for her, for the funeral procession tomorrow. It seemed strange; did she mean what she said?"

"I think so. She had a visitor this afternoon who brought her much comfort. I think she will be able to face the journey tomorrow."

"Who was it?"

"Domina Chloe Aemilia."

"Caius Aemilius's sister? Well, we must let bygones be bygones if she can work such a miracle."

"Not Chloe," I thought, as I went through the empty dining-room to the moonlit terrace beyond. Dion was curled up on the seat.

"Chloe came," I said. "May I sit down, or I shan't keep awake."

"Don't, Timandra." There was a sudden pain in his voice. "It's dark here, and we've both got news to tell. The moment I saw Nerea I knew that something had happened."

I told him quickly. It was always easier to speak to Dion in the dark. Chloe would say he was my brother, but that did not help when I had to talk to him every day before others remembering I was a slave.

"Did Chloe heal her completely?" he asked.

"I don't think so. She started something, or rather, something started because she was there. Now tell me. You found Timotheos?"

"Timas the tilemaker!" There was laughter in his voice. "Yes, I found him, brick-red with clay dust, because I was impatient and went early. Everyone seemed to know him, for I was waved through the outer shop and workroom to a yard at the back with a clay pit and a kiln, and rows of drying racks. A couple of men with legs like treetrunks were treading clay, and Timas was cutting it in slabs like dough and ramming them into moulds for the curly tiles that go at the corner of a roof. I watched him for half an hour before they finished the batch, and he was really working, stripped down to the most awful rags and sweating like a galley slave. They were all singing, though, to keep time."

"Why must he work like that?"

"He told me afterwards when the man in charge, Drusus I suppose, came through and said they could knock off. I helped him wash at the water trough and when he was clean and presentable we went for a walk to that little garden above the new theatre. Timas said that although he came to Corinth this time to help Apollos—he was here once before, two years ago—he always works wherever he goes so that he isn't a burden on the brothers. Most of them are poor."

"Why didn't you take him to the baths?"

"I suggested it, but he said he's been circumcised and that sometimes made it awkward. It would in Corinth, I can see that."

"Tell me everything he said."

Dion laughed. "By then I should be asleep, even if you weren't. Oh, we can keep the scrolls. Timandra, I feel as if someone had said 'All your life you have been looking at the back of the picture, now let me turn it round for you and show you what the colours are really like.' Timas was about my age when he met Paulus, and he said it made him feel as I do now. He was used to going to the synagogue in Lystra where he lived with his mother, his father was dead by then. But the first time he saw Paulus it was outside the city when he was out for a walk with a friend, and a cripple who was as much a part of the city gates as the hinges on the doors suddenly got up off his pad of rags and walked. It looked as if it was Paulus who had done it, only Timas saw at once that there must be more to it than that, but the awful thing was that there was a riot. At first the crowd thought that Paulus and his friend were new gods themselves and then when they realized that they weren't they stoned them. Paulus was nearly killed and had to leave Lystra at once, and it was only later when he was able to come back that Timas first met him at the synagogue and found out what was behind the power that had healed the cripple. That waiting must have been awful."

"What did Paulus tell him?"

"I can't explain it the way Timas did. But imagine, Timandra, we've talked about a God who was a creator of everything; now, let me get this right. We think we know some of the ways things work in the world—that if we plant corn in the ground and the weather is right it will come up and grow; and that when the wind comes from the north in the winter it brings the cold. How if this creating God made men to work in a certain way, but left them to find it out for themselves because that was all part of the pattern? We can see that most of them haven't understood and have done things all wrong. If you were God what would you do then?"

"I should want to start all over again, but I don't suppose you mean that. He would have to show them, I suppose."

"How could he do that?"

"Don't make me guess, Dion. I'm too tired to think straight."

"I'm sorry. But would men understand if there was one man who was sent by God, who did do things the right way, as God had meant them to be?"

"Surely, if they once saw it, and it all worked."

"If only you were right! Because, Timandra, Timas said the man did come, fifty years ago in Judea, and the procurator crucified him for stirring up trouble. But he was more than just a man, he was God's firstborn son, part of him."

"They crucified a son of God, come to earth as they did in the old stories?" It was strange and horrible, not what I had been expecting at all; I remembered Nerea and the crucifixion that had so marked her.

"Yes, Timas said he did die because he was a real man, with a body that could get tired and be hurt, but because he was God's son death couldn't hold him. He rose from a closed tomb after three days, he's still alive, he is with everyone who believes in him, Paulus and Timas and Chloe. He is the 'Lord' they were praying to at the house of Titus. It's as if the gate of life was shut and he's opened it to us from the inside. His name is the password we can enter by."

"The name of a son of God who was stronger than death, no wonder there is power!" I breathed. "But what were the rules man got wrong, that I suppose we break every hour of the day or the world wouldn't be such a terrible place? Why did the procurator try to kill him?"

"The rule is love, which is too simple for most people to see, and very, very dangerous. People are so frightened by love, they don't understand it and it makes them feel uncomfortable." He yawned enormously. "Timas has another scroll, very precious, that he'll lend me next time I meet him. It has some of the words the Lord, the son of God, spoke when he was living with us. Timas says I can copy what I have time for."

"When will you see him again?"

"In two days, after the funeral. Oh, Timandra, did she only die today?"

So that was how it was that Nerea went to the funeral of Olympias. She came home tear-stained and shaken, but that was how anyone would have felt. Then there were several quiet days. I hoped each morning when I woke to find Nerea silent and withdrawn that Chloe would come, but she did not. Dion went twice more to the Street of the Tilemakers, and once to a meeting held early in the morning at the house of Titus. Each time he returned to tell me what he had seen and heard, and even more than by his eager and sometimes incoherent explanations I felt my own mind being changed by the conviction that seemed to shine in his face. It was as if he was in love for the first time and he was coming home to pour out each detail of the beauty and lovableness of his girl in the nearest sympathetic ear.

As I watched him I wished sometimes that it had been some girl he had found, because I was beginning to see that the future as a follower of the Way would be far more difficult for him than for me, and yet, as I had said on the night of the first meeting, it had to be something that could hold us both. I thought of the picture he had drawn of the well-born Timas working like a slave in the clay-pits. Did I want something like this for him? Then I remembered the easy and unattractive arrogance of Secundus, and so many of the young men I saw as I went about in the streets and markets of Corinth. Which was the better way for a young man to live? Which came nearer to the pattern that this half-known son of God had set when he lived as a man? This was something that it was not easy to discuss with Dion, and I had no other way of knowing, except from the unwilling conviction that was growing in my heart.

The household gradually settled into a new pattern. The baby was four months old and sleeping through the night, and my warning about a wet-nurse had proved true, for Nerea's milk had gone with the shock of Olympias's death. Urbinus brought in a decent girl, the wife of an attendant at the baths, with a young baby herself, who was glad to live in the house for a few months and feed them both. She was a nice girl, and a devoted mother, and I was glad that there was someone else to leave Pyrrha with, for Hegiso was now completely unreliable.

CHLOE

Nerea moved back from the small room next door to where I still slept with the baby, to her husband's room on the other side of the courtyard. She seemed quite well now in her body, recovered from the ordeal of her daughter's difficult birth, though quieter and older. She had not left the house again since the funeral.

Then Chloe came again at last. It was on a day that had been difficult for all of us; another member of the city council had been charged with a considerable injustice connected with the guardianship of a young ward. It seemed as if this time the city was concerned that an important case should be tried with exact regard to the law, after the tragedy of Vipsanius. Urbinus was to speak in defence of the accused man before the proconsul, and all day we had been waiting for news of how the case had gone. I had not often seen my master nervous before, but he had been tense and strained when he left the house that morning, for this success or failure would be important to him politically.

When Chloe was announced late in the afternoon Nerea was delighted to see her.

"Oh, it's so good to have someone to talk to, I didn't know how to get through the next two hours," she said, jumping up to greet her older guest and spilling her embroidery on to the warm paving stones under the fig tree.

I ran to fetch wine, cool from the flagon hanging in the well. Then I sat a little way off with Metella while the ladies talked. Chloe stayed a long time, till the shadows were lengthening and the swallows swooping lower, for Nerea seemed unwilling to let her leave.

"Do come again soon," she said, like a child whose toy is being taken away, when Chloe made her farewells at last.

"Won't you come to visit me?" asked Chloe, smiling at her eagerness.

"Oh," Nerea stopped dead, in her leisurely walk towards

the atrium with her guest. "But it isn't easy to leave the house just now, my husband . . ." Her voice trailed away, but Chloe must have noticed as I had that it was not the flat refusal she would have made a month before.

"Perhaps in two days' time, when all this excitement is over, I could come for you with a chair. We don't live far away, and that would be easy for a first visit."

Nothing more was said, but I was hopeful. Metella pressed my hand before she hurried after her mistress. "We pray every day for all of you, and your master's brother," she whispered.

Urbinus Torquartus came back to his home that evening the hero of the hour, and Dion came back drunk. They were not alone, half the council seemed to be with them, anxious to be seen with the man who had won his case in such a masterly way. The master paused first to make an offering at the family shrine, and then he moved among his guests who seemed to fill every room and courtyard in the house, while we were kept busy with cups of wine and things to eat.

Dion had come in with an arm round the shoulders of Nicolaus, who had not been to the house for two months, and surrounded by a group of older friends. He was flushed and excited and very good-looking, after a fashion which I had never found attractive. It was hard for me to believe, in the glimpses I had of him as I hurried backwards and forwards to the kitchen, that he was the same young man who had stood with me by the dying Olympias's bed. I could have wept with my half-understood doubts and disappointments, and I was glad that Timas and his other new friends could not see him.

The street outside the house was bright as day with torches when the guests left, but the house was untidy and smelled of perfume and spilled wine. We cleared the worst of the mess away, Nerea trailed happily over to the far side of the court-yard, and it seemed strange to help her prepare for bed and undo the elaborate curls of her party hairstyle in a different room, without Pyrrha asleep close by in her cradle.

When I left her the house was quiet and a few lamps were still burning. Urbinus and Rufus came through from the main entrance. Dion had disappeared, but there was a light in his room. Hegiso or no Hegiso, I knew I would not be able to sleep until I had seen him again.

He was lying across his bed fully dressed. He seemed to be asleep, but he was flushed and uncomfortable, twisted in the heavy folds of his toga, which had wine stains down the front that the fuller would be hard put to get out. I unlaced his sandals and he moved and grunted as my fingers tickled him; that made it easier to get the toga loose. He was going to feel terrible in the morning, or perhaps sooner, I thought, as I moved a basin and a jug of water over to the head of his bed where he could reach them. Really he needed washing, for his hands were sticky and his tunic was damp with sweat, but that I would not do for him. As I stood for a last moment, looking down with a mixture of dismay and affection, he opened his eyes.

"Oh, Jupiter!" he gasped, and flopped over towards the basin.

I left him to go through the next hours alone.

9 · TWO VISITORS

The curtain still hung over the door of Dion's room next morning, as I helped the other slaves collect the last of the winecups left by guests among the roots of the fig tree and in the pots with the climbing roses. Nerea was also sleeping late, and the whole house was quiet. I was still tired myself, and it was difficult not to snap at Rhodippe when she came to me with questions about dinner which I could not answer. If I managed to seem calm, I felt inside like a bird with muddy and ruffled feathers, yet a quiet voice seemed to say that I knew very well that a quarrel now would help no one—as it never did.

I did not notice Dion go out. It must have been while I was getting Nerea's midday meal. When I left Pyrrha with the wet-nurse to see if anything in his room needed clearing away I met Rufus in the doorway.

He gave me an amused smile. "Our boy's a man now. It's all right, Timandra, I've cleared up the mess."

The room still smelt sour, and his smile upset me. "Do you think it's behaving like a man to get drunk?"

"Most men do."

"I know they do, but that doesn't make it right." The sickening memory of that same smell in the courtyard of Corvus's house came over me like a suddenly remembered bad dream. It was a long time since I had felt it so strongly.

He patted me on the shoulder, kind but awkward. "It's not for us to worry about, and he's regretting it now. Dion isn't another baby for you to fuss over."

I knew he wasn't, but that didn't stop me caring about him. Something had gone wrong again for Dion during the last day, and that mattered very much, for the Way must be true for everything that his life brought him, or it could not be true for me.

Nerea did not miss Dion until the evening meal. "He may not be hungry, he was ill last night," I said.

She took that to mean that he was lying down in his room and told Urbinus so. No one went to look, and it was late before I was sure myself that Dion had not come back. Whether he had gone to his old friends or his new, I did not think we should find him even if we searched, so I told no one.

He came back at midday on the second day, with dust caked on his sandals and dark marks round his eyes. Nerea was dressing to receive Chloe, pretty and excited as a normal young woman would be at the prospect of an outing. There was no time for me to follow Dion to his room, and anyway I knew that this time I must not, or I would really seem like a fussy nurse.

Chloe came, and in the flutter of greeting her Dion came out again, clean and tidy. He greeted the visitor politely, managing not to make it obvious to Nerea that he had met Chloe before.

"Dion, would the chatter of women bore you, or will you come with us to my house?" asked Chloe as we were about to leave. She had brought two chairs, with light side curtains, more to keep out the dust than for privacy, not like the closed litters Nerea had travelled in before.

"I should be glad to come and listen while you talk. I slept badly last night, as I'm afraid you can see," he said with a rueful laugh. "I've been with my brother and his friends lately so much that I've almost forgotten the social side of life."

"Will you walk beside me?" asked Nerea, hanging back in the doorway.

"Of course, and here's Rufus to attend you as well. I don't think Urbinus needs him today."

Rufus, who no doubt had had other urgent things planned for the afternoon, saw Nerea's frightened face, and the gestures I was making to him behind her back. He had said that he would believe in any god who could make his mistress normal; now was his time to see how far that work had already gone.

There was room for the two chairs and the slaves who carried them to walk side by side down the wide Laechium road, but Rufus kept close behind with me, so that Nerea would know herself surrounded with friends. Chloe rode with her curtains back on both sides. As we passed out of the city gate and the road was less crowded and noisy she stretched across and drew back the inside curtain of Nerea's chair.

"There, isn't it a beautiful day? Look at the waters of the Gulf, I wish I had a robe that colour."

Nerea's hands had tightened on the sides of the chair till her knuckles were white, but she raised her eyes slowly to see a wider view than for many a year, down the steep road through the olive groves and little farms to the western port of the city and the brilliant waters beyond, turquoise shading to emerald in the deep places. The wind caught the soft hair on her forehead and lifted it, and there was a freshness in the air in spite of the heat, after the stuffy summer months in a house inside the city walls. Nerea's grasp loosened.

"Look, there's our house, away to the left behind the cypresses."

Nerea put up her hand and drew back the left-hand curtain herself.

Chloe's home was large and untidy-looking, part farm, part villa. Built over the ruins of another destroyed long before when the legions occupied Greece, it had the beautiful mosaic floors of the former owner, but somehow the new rooms did not quite fit them, so that in places the edges of elaborate patterns of blue or red and ochre stones disappeared under side walls. However, Chloe took us quickly over the goddesses of the atrium, and Europa and the bull in the central room of the house, and out on to a terrace looking north, shaded by a vine trellis. The leaves were already beginning to curl and wither, and the unripe fruit hung heavy above us like swarming clusters of green bees.

Nerea arranged herself on a cushioned bench and smiled at Chloe. "What a lovely place! Did I ever come here as a child? I think I remember it as if I'd seen it before in a dream."

She seemed quite happy. I put her fan where she could reach it and saw that Metella was bringing cool drinks. Dion had gone a little way down the terrace, out of sight from where Nerea was sitting. I was wondering whether to follow him when he beckoned to me.

I could tell nothing from his face. He still looked pale even after the walk in the hot sun, and thinner; surely one day could not have done that? And I knew that Rufus had been right, and that he was no longer the boy he had been when I first came to the house. Then I saw red clay dust under the nails of hands that were usually very clean, and I knew where he had been.

"You went to Timas," I said.

He looked down at his hands and smiled. "I must go to the baths on the way home! Yes, I went to Timas, but that was afterwards. I went to Nicolaus first."

"Oh Dion!"

"Why did you never like him?"

"Don't you know yet?"

"I suppose I wouldn't have done till yesterday. Yes, I do see now. Grandmother didn't like him either. Did you come to my room two nights ago? I couldn't remember if I'd really seen you or not before I started being sick."

"Yes, I put you to bed, as far as anyone did."

"I'm sorry, I was hoping you hadn't seen. Now I know why you've been looking at me so thoughtfully for the last hour!"

"Rufus said getting drunk was part of growing up!"

"He's right in a way, but that was what Nicolaus said. You see, the trial was really very exciting, Timandra, and when it was over I was suddenly not just a schoolboy waiting for his grown-up toga next month, and then two years at the school of Simonides before I go into the government service. I was the brother of the coming man, and it felt very nice indeed. I was proud of Urbinus again because I knew that he'd worked hard and it had been very clever to get old Pollio acquitted, and I was sure he was innocent. I forgot all about how I'd felt when Vipsanius was killed, and what happened at the workshop of Asyncritus, and I found I was drinking with Nicolaus and his friends and enjoying it very much. Being a man seemed exciting and—free—in a way I hadn't imagined."

"Did you remember Timas?"

"Yes, and after the third cup of wine, the idea of him slaving in a clay-pit seemed quite ridiculous. The evil one is very clever, Timandra."

"And that's how you were feeling when you came home?"

"I must have looked very silly because I wasn't used to drinking, and I know I did some foolish things."

"You looked horrible, like Secundus when he's drunk. I'm sorry, I shouldn't have said that."

"I'm glad you did, it gives me a very good picture. Well then, of course, I was sick, and I lay there for hours with the bed feeling a little way beneath me and rocking so that I couldn't sleep. I heard the cocks crow and the watch go round before I finally went off. But I'd promised to meet Nicolaus and the others at the gymnasium before midday, so I had to get up earlier than I wanted to. I hadn't been there for a long time and it seemed like coming back home, except that I still felt ill. They were all there, but somehow they didn't look so friendly. We just sat about. No one was doing any proper training, they were just talking as we always did I suppose, only it sounded different.

"Then Nicolaus's brother said, 'It's a month since I saw you, Dion. Who's your new love, she must be surpassingly beautiful to keep you from your friends. Or is it that dark-haired freedman I saw you with five days ago in the street behind the new basilica?'"

"Timas?"

"It must have been. He said a lot of other things that I won't repeat, and all the time I was seeing that I had got a new love, not athletics or philosophy or Timas, though I do love him in a way they wouldn't understand. I suppose I love life itself, or the Lord behind all life, the master whom Timas serves. I just got up and walked away. It was midday when I got to Drusus's shop and Timas was still working, so I stripped off and helped him till he'd finished. He seemed to understand why because he didn't ask questions. I've been with him ever since. I feel as if I'd been ill, and I'm not quite over it yet, but I know what I don't want, and that's something."

I was so happy that I thought I was going to cry, and I could see Dion felt the same himself, because he turned away quickly before I could speak, though actually I could not think of anything to say. Then Nerea called me.

"Come and sit down here, you must be tired after the walk." I was glad to sit on a low stool and sort embroidery threads with my head bent, till I felt calmer.

Dion came back too, and Rufus approached shyly from the garden, where he had been examining a newly planted terrace with Chloe's overseer. Metella took him a cup of wine and he sat down a little way away from us. It was wonderfully peaceful, with the ladies talking of nothing very much, and the faint farm and garden noises of distant animals, and water running, and the wind in the vine leaves.

Nerea put down the sewing she had brought with her. "I'm so glad I came. I've never lived outside the city, is that why it seems so peaceful?"

Chloe smiled across at her. "Peace comes from the inside, not the outside. I'm happy, and I think my household are." The girl Metella looked up from her work and smiled.

"And where does your peace come from?" asked Nerea, still in the light voice of a woman making conversation.

"From my God," said Chloe quietly.

"Is there a new God in the city then? Where has he been brought from this time?" asked Nerea, still not serious.

Chloe put back her head and laughed. "Yes, my dear, I suppose you could say there was a new God, or one came three years ago from Syria, and that's not for the first time. If any God can ever be new, and mine is older than the world, for he made it."

"Chloe, you're serious?"

"My dear, should I joke about my life, or what kept me alive after my husband died, and Lucilla?"

"Do you know which God she's talking about?" Nerea was puzzled and she turned to Dion.

Before us all he said, "Yes, I know, or I'm beginning to know. And it's true, dear Nerea, that there is a new God in Corinth and he comes with power."

"Is he worshipped then? How is it that I haven't heard of him?"

"Perhaps because you never went out where other people talk about such things. Olympias knew him, but she did not think you would have listened if she spoke to you. But perhaps now you are stronger, you would come with me to hear more about him? He comes with a power and a joy and a peace that you have never dreamed of." Chloe's face was still grave, but it seemed lit from behind.

"I don't know . . . yes, I think I should like that, if my husband gave me leave. Dion?"

"I have met the worshippers of this God already, so has Timandra," he said.

"Am I the only one who does not understand?" She looked around her with surprise.

Then Rufus came forward. "No, my lady, but if this is the God Domina Olympias believed in, then I will come with you."

On the way back to the city we made plans, and I was walking in a happy dream at the thought of my mistress, and all those in the household of Urbinus that I loved, singing together with the joy I had once seen.

I think that was when I first really came to love Nerea, for the sweetness and simplicity with which she had accepted the strangeness of what she had been told, when she could have been angered by what might have seemed a conspiracy.

And yet the days passed and the hoped-for meeting did not take place. First it was because Pyrrha had a summer fever, and although the child was quickly over it she had never been ill before and Nerea fretted. Then Secundus sickened too, for it was the end of the long hot weather when there was always illness in the city. Again he was soon well, but he came home for a time, excused from duty till our cooking and more sleep than he allowed himself at the officers' quarters put back the spring in his step. We were now within a few days of the ceremony when Dion would receive his toga of manhood and be entered in the records of his clan and of the city. On the day itself there was the customary family party and visits to be paid.

It was not long after, at the beginning of the autumn, that

Timas came to the house. Rufus, who did not know him, left him in the atrium and came to me because Dion was out. It was only the second time I had seen Timas, but through Dion I seemed to know him very well, and when he smiled in greeting it gave me the same shock that it had before.

Timas is still the only man I have ever known that I could have loved with all the abandonment of the heroine of one of the old plays, but I thank God that I knew even at the beginning that what I felt must remain small and closed inside my heart, or I would lose what he was able to be to me. And that has been something rich and precious, an older brother given to a lonely child.

"I hoped to find Dion," he said, when he had greeted me. "Tomorrow is the first day of the week for us, the first day of seven because we keep it in memory of the Lord's coming back from death, not the old Jewish last day of seven. I know Dion has been busy these last few days, but I was hoping that tomorrow he could be with us."

There was a feeling of excitement behind what he was saying, that was strong enough to come across to me. "Why, will something special happen then?"

"Yes, there's been a letter to Titus from Paulus my teacher. We shall read it tomorrow. Phoebe, who lives in Chenchraea, brought it up this morning. It's only four days since the teacher wrote it in Ephesus, so close that I can almost hear his voice in the words!"

Dion came in and his eyes lit up at the sight of Timas, even though he looked tired.

Timas greeted him with "Peace, brother," and they clasped hands. I saw that they were indeed brothers, more nearly related than Dion was to Secundus in everything except blood. Timas explained why he had come.

"Yes, of course I can be free tomorrow," said Dion. "Timandra, you should come with us."

I said nothing, for my time was not my own, and he understood at once. "Is Nerea dressed for company?" he asked.

I had left her in the garden waiting for Urbinus to come home for dinner. "Will you ask her if she will receive my friend?" he said.

Wondering, I went on ahead. Urbinus must have come in by the side door, for he was already there, talking to his wife in the fading evening light, when I reached the garden. However, Dion was close behind me.

"Nerea, this is my friend Timotheos son of Ariston from Lystra." I stood back in the shadows of the portico, watching, but too far away to hear what was being said. Urbinus, I could see, had quickly satisfied himself that Timas came from a good family and in that light would not have noticed his work-roughened hands. Nerea was being shy but gracious; I knew her well enough to be certain that she would like Timas much better than Dion's last friend Nicolaus.

Urbinus called for Rufus, and Timas sat down with the family group. Rufus passed me carrying a taper to light the first lamps; when he came back he said "One extra for dinner!"

An hour later, as I cleared away the last of the dishes and Rufus poured wine for the men, I remembered the first time I had waited on my mistress in the same room. And tonight she was wearing the same rose-coloured dress, but she seemed taller and less rounded, quiet, a woman after the difficult summer.

Dion, whose fair head had been bent close on the same couch to Timas's dark one, pushed himself higher on his elbow.

"Nerea, the various fevers prevented us from accepting Chloe's invitation to go with her to learn about her God. Timas has come with the same invitation. Will you come with us tomorrow, early? You can leave Pyrrha now, can't you?"

Something crossed Nerea's face, a hope and then a quick memory. "In the morning, no, not at the moment, Dion. I will come, I know my husband would permit it——" she looked at Urbinus under her lashes, "But it will be a little while before I can come."

Then she glanced across and saw my face. I had not known I was showing so plainly what I was thinking. "Of course you may take Timandra, as I can see that it so clearly is her wish."

Urbinus smiled kindly but with no understanding of what was going on, and Secundus was frankly puzzled. However, he asked no questions.

The small pang of regret that I felt because Nerea would not be with us was lost in joy at what now lay ahead. I hardly noticed that evening why it was that my mistress would not come.

10 · THE LIGHT BEYOND DARKNESS

Although it was still dark between the tall houses of Corinth when we left home, the sun was flaming rose and gold high up behind the clouds piled to the east. Like a tent for the sun, when it rises, I thought, humming the hymn to myself as I walked. A cool wind came from the sea, blowing the leaves and rubbish in the unswept street about the legs of the first people going to market, and the small boys, still half-asleep as they walked to school. It was the first time I had worn a cloak since the spring, but I was glad of it as I followed two paces behind Dion, with Rufus beside me.

Rufus was there because he had said he would come, but I could see that he was puzzled and uncomfortable. He had seen the beginning of a change in Nerea, but that change was not yet complete and I think he felt that he had almost been trapped into coming with us, but was too honest a man not to keep to his word.

Dion waited for us at the corner of the narrow street behind the basilica. The door of Titus's house was open and men were going in ahead of us. From inside there came light and the sound of singing. For a moment I hesitated, frightened that something that had once been marvellous could not be so again; I looked along the narrow street over the roofs to the eastern crest of Acrocorinth, tipped with walls and temples. The sky there was blue and a golden light just touched those high roofs as I turned into the house.

It was crowded already, with men standing in the doorway of the inner room and children sitting on the floor. It was clear that the meeting had begun long before dawn, for there was already a glow, a brightness, on most of the faces there, like the first light of the sun I had seen a moment before.

I dropped my cloak, for the air was warm with bodies and the smell of the lamps which still burned. Dion put an arm round me and led me between the standing people to a place not far from the centre of the room, where Titus and Timas and the other elders were sitting. Timas saw us, and his eyes lit up in welcome. He gave the scroll he was holding to the man who sat beside him and came to us. Rufus was behind us, quiet among the singing people. Timas kissed Dion and then me, and stretched out a hand to him; Rufus took it with a puzzled smile.

I have tried before to make words describe what is beyond words. It is as easy as gathering up the short threads when you have finished an embroidery and saying, 'Now you know what the pattern is like'. When I tell Pyrrha about it she will not find it strange, because she has seen what happened then many times since she was a small child, but she will not be able to imagine how it was to come to it freshly without knowing what to expect. Dion took something different from that morning's worship, but for me from the first moment when the singing surrounded and welcomed us, everything was a confirmation of something I had already accepted. I was ignorant, I knew I was accepting something and someone I did not understand, but I had no more power than a girl in love has, when a man she hardly knows takes her hands and says, 'Come', to resist and ask careful questions first.

I suppose we had been there an hour before the letter was

read, although I had no knowledge of time, except to notice that light now poured in through the upper windows and most of the lamps had been put out. We sat on the floor among the children, for it was a long letter. Timas read it in a voice that was not always steady, and from time to time he paused as small murmurs of agreement or joy came from the close-packed listeners. Chloe was on a bench across the room, Dion's shoulder against mine, and the words I did not fully understand poured into my heart.

"Because God in his mercy has given us the work to do which brings us among you," read Timas, "we don't lose heart. We have given up using devious ways to persuade people, when we state the truth openly every man can weigh in his own conscience the truth of our words against his own knowledge of God. If the good news we bring still seems obscure to people it is because the evil one has so blinded them that they cannot tell light from darkness when they see it. Our light is the wonderful glory of Jesus; when we see him we see God. We are not teaching you out of our own knowledge, but we are bringing you to Jesus; we are your servants so that we can bring you to him. Our God said, 'Let light shine out of darkness' and he shone in our hearts to show us the glorious light of his Son."

"Jesus, Jesus," a man beside me breathed softly over and over again.

Timas paused and looked around him. I knew that what came next had moved him deeply. Then he smiled. "We are like old pottery jars in which someone has hidden a valuable treasure, so that it may be quite clear that the precious power we have comes from God and not ourselves. We are surrounded by difficulties but not crushed by them, puzzled but not driven to despair, attacked but not left friendless, knocked to the ground but not destroyed. We always carry around with us the memory of Jesus's death for us, so that his rising to life may show through us. In the Hebrew writings a poet wrote, 'I believed and so I spoke'. We have something which we believe in, and so we speak, because we know that the God who raised his son from death, will bring us, together with you, through death to his presence."

My mind was held there, in this perfect trust that the teacher had in his God. I remembered so much that Timas had told Dion about Paulus, for the love he had for him showed through his every word.

"What does he look like?" Dion had asked. "He must be a wonderful speaker, like Apollos."

Timas had crowed with laughter. "Paulus? No! He's a little man, rather beaten-down looking except that he has piercing eyes. It's not surprising after the life he's led for the last fifteen years. I forget how often he's been flogged between Antioch and Achaia for making trouble. They nearly beat him here in Corinth! And his words don't flow as Apollos's do, I don't think they need to. They're true and you know it, and that's what helps people to believe. But if you met him in the street or on his travels you'd just think he was a small Jewish teacher and not notice him."

And what he believes about his dying and living God has brought him to all that, I thought. Not that there haven't been dying and living Gods before, but did they have the power to take the fear from the heart of a hurt girl or give speech to a dying woman? O Lord my rock and my redeemer.

Then I remembered another, earlier dawn over the sea, and the small Jewish teacher who had spoken those words to an unknown child with sincerity and simplicity. And I knew that I too had spoken with Paulus.

I bent my head and cried. The rest of the letter went unheard, while Dion put an arm round me, not understanding but trying to comfort me and listen at the same time.

I had asked a blind, blank heaven, when my father died, for

something larger than my own life to hold to and live by and make my own, and I was being offered the core of life itself. What price must I pay to possess it? Was it something within my power to give? All that I had heard was true and I knew I was not worthy of it. I was a slave and my living was not my own that I could give it joyfully back to my Lord like Timas or Paulus; and I was a woman, I must always watch from the border of life.

Suddenly I was aware of silence around me, and then of loving prayer made by many voices, one after the other, for Paulus and to the God who had sent him. Then there was singing again, and I was outside it like a child who tries to peer through the cracks in the door of a lighted room. When Dion stood up to sing I pulled away from him and stayed kneeling on the floor with my face buried in my hands. I did not know how they had come out of the roaring and evil darkness that now held me away from that light. I had never killed or enslaved another, but all the small and large unkindnesses and selfishnesses of my own life were now in my heart a part of a larger evil that even so loving a God could not forgive.

Then the room was quiet again. Someone had taken me gently by the shoulders and I heard Timas's voice. "Sister, you are in distress. Let us help you."

I had reached the stage in crying of a child whose voice cannot come through the sobbing. "But it's true, all of it, I'm certain. But I can't be a part of it. I'm a slave. What can I give when I don't own myself?"

There were other people round me now, the elder Titus, kind faces that I did not know, and Dion—very white, feeling through me what it must be to be his brother's slave. Then an arm from behind drew me back against a man's tunic with the sound of a heart beating fast beneath it.

Rufus said, "But she won't always be a slave. We've got a good master, he freed me."

"Brother, she is free already, if she will only believe it. She has been bought for a far greater price than your master could ever ask, for the price of a life. He could kill her and not separate her from her true Lord. Timandra, do you love him? Do you believe he is God's son and that he has come back through death with the power to make your life new?"

I pushed Rufus gently back. He was kind but he had not understood, and Timas had. The silence seemed to go on for a very long time, like the dark tunnel of a nightmare when the light at the end is almost invisible and does not come nearer. Close to my heart a voice said, "But this is ridiculous, to speak like this and cry before so many strangers, what can a God be like who expects this of you?" And then another voice came, much stronger, infinitely understanding, the voice of Olympias. "What if God asked something of you that seemed small and ridiculous? You say you would die for a faith, would you speak for one?"

Dear Olympias. I opened my mouth and no voice came, then with an effort that felt like a tremendous shout and came out soft and small like a child with a difficult confession to make, I said, "Jesus, I believe in you. Thank you. I know you love me. Jesus, Jesus." And then I was out of the tunnel and the sun had risen, and the glory of that sunrise is beyond light or sound or colour. Pyrrha must come to it for herself, for it is beyond the power of any man to give it to another. There were hands on my head. I stretched up to touch them, and I sang and there were no words, but only light like the lacing beams of the sun coming from behind storm clouds, as I had known it before. Other voices sang with me, till the sound was a crown of light.

As it faded away Timas helped me to my feet and gave me back to my friends. People made room for me so that I was sitting on a bench holding Dion's hand. I could feel that there was something still running through me, a pulse that was an echo of the light and the singing, and I wondered if he could feel it through me. When I could, I slipped loose for long enough to tuck my hair back under my veil and wipe my tear-wet face and running nose; then I slipped my hand back confidently into his again. The Lord's peace was around me, strong and steady, like the warmth of the risen sun. Dion was a part of it, but when I looked at him I saw that I had gone on ahead to a place he was not yet ready for.

The meeting ended. Chloe came and kissed me, and there were many others, faces and half-remembered names, and shy joy and simple friendliness. When almost everyone had gone Timas came back from his own goodbyes.

"Come through here with me," he said. "I must talk to you."

He led us through a door at the back of the room into a paved courtyard, built between high walls. The sun was just high enough now to reach the south-east corner where there was a climbing rose and a stone bench. Timas made me sit down between Dion and himself, while Rufus, still not part of what he saw, leaned back against the tall urn that held a small white oleander bush.

"So our Lord took you to himself, Timandra. It's wonderful, isn't it? But are you certain what you've done?"

I laughed, it seemed the most beautiful and natural thing in the world that I who did not own my own body or the veil that covered me, could give myself away so freely.

"No, I don't understand, how could I? And I don't need to. If this was right—and it was—then the rest must follow."

Timas smiled. "When it happened to me I felt as if I'd been a blocked spring, and someone had cleaned me so that the water could gush out fresh and strong. That's how it happens. God came into you today, and if the spring is kept clean he will flow through you to other people. It will be difficult, it will be a battle that lasts as long as you live, but what is there in life that can be worth so much? And when we can we must seal you with water for your new life. God has already given you one baptism in his own time, often it comes after the water, but that is something that we can't arrange."

"Doesn't it matter that Timandra's still a slave?" asked Rufus.

"If she had been free would she have ever come to your house? Would she have met you or Olympias? In the Lord's purpose he could have reached out to her another way, but like this it has brought blessing to you all. Timandra, I asked you if you knew what you had done, but don't ever forget that before you chose your master today he had chosen you. If you let him, he will show you a day at a time what that choosing was for."

"Then has he chosen me too?" Dion's voice was light and hesitant.

"Don't you know? What has he told you in your heart?"

I was sitting between the two young men. I felt the force, the longing that went out from Timas, the tension in Dion, still locked within his own darkness.

"Timas," I said, "it's different for Dion. Won't his life be very changed if he follows the Way? You didn't expect to be part wandering teacher part tilemaker when you were a schoolboy, did you? And your family didn't expect it either."

Timas hooted with laughter. "I hadn't got any practical ideas when Paulus came to Lystra, I was still going to be a poet." Then he was serious. "My father had died by then, perhaps that made it easier, but we must face, all of us, that when we open this door which we have never opened before, and set out down a new road, we don't know where it will take us. Perhaps round and back to our own front door—we may already be where the master needs us. But no way can be as difficult as staying where he doesn't want us to be."

"Then there may be danger in this," said Rufus. "Your

Paulus has been in prison and often punished; and what you say could set a woman against her husband or a son against his father. Can that be right? The Emperor won't like it!"

"Bother the Emperor, and my father's already dead," said Dion. "Timandra, it isn't easier for you, I think it's the same for everyone. It's just that I'm not ready yet; when I am, whatever it costs, I won't be able to help myself. If it's not like that then it won't be true."

Timas stood up, and we rose with him; the sun was shining clear down into the little court now and the morning was well on.

"The master's timing is perfect," he said. "But I've been praying that you should come to him soon. You see, Paulus wants me with him in Ephesus for the winter, and already the sailing season's almost over. I may not even be here for the next first day if there's still a ship at Chenchraea sailing east."

Dion took him by both his arms and shook him. "Timas, you can't."

"No? I would have told you before if I'd known, but the letter came with the other one yesterday. Paulus isn't well and there's so much only he can do and write. I can be eyes and hands and feet for him. I can listen when he speaks and write it down because I know his mind so well."

"You'll be like a secretary?"

"Yes, something like. I love to serve Paulus, probably more than I should do because I find it very hard to go away from him. Then when I do, I meet people like you, and now it will be very hard to tear free and leave Corinth, but it's not the sort of pain I would ever want to avoid. And I never have to leave the Master."

"Will you ever come back?"

We had walked almost as far as the door into the house. Suddenly I saw that this was an end as final as walking up the gangplank from Samos had been. We three, and Rufus, would not stand here together again. Months and years ahead if we met we would be different people. There was pain in the thought, but also a kind of wonder, that every part of life could be so full of meaning. The parting would be hardest for Dion.

"I can't choose how things happen," Timas spoke again. "Timandra, I wish I could be near you during the next months; you know they won't be easy and there may be some very unexpected things in them for you, but you will have many wise councillors here in Corinth. There's Chloe and Titus and the elders; keep very close to them."

"If I can find someone to take the letter, I'll write to you," said Dion.

"Oh, that would be wonderful." Timas's face was full of a quick joy. "If I can, I'll see you to say goodbye—if not, 'Go with God'."

11 · "GO WITH GOD"

Next morning when I went to her early, Nerea was sick, before she had time to get up. After I had bathed her face and made her comfortable again she looked up at me, her eyes dark and frightened in a pale, drained face.

"Timandra, it can't be!"

"It's very soon, Pyrrha's barely six months. When should you be sure?"

"In about ten days. Don't tell anyone, please. Not yet."

I wanted to sit down and put my arms round her, but Nerea would not accept that from me, not yet. Could it be right for her to have another child so soon, after her difficult first labour? I knew that although her strength had returned there were still times when backache troubled her. I wanted to tell Dion, it was hard keeping anything from him, and Chloe even more; she would be practical and helpful in so many ways, but I must do as Nerea had asked me.

She kept me very close to her during the next few days, and with care we were able to disguise the attacks of sickness that came nearly every morning. Urbinus we barely saw till late afternoon each day; he was quite absorbed in his duties, and by the time he came home his wife was well enough to lie on a couch for dinner, eating very little, but smiling and listening.

What gave me very great joy was that she seemed to want to

144

hear all that had happened at the meeting on the morning my darkness had ended.

"I've heard of people feeling like that," she said, "when they were received into one of the mysteries, but never so simply, or through a new God people haven't heard about. I wish I could come myself, but at the moment that isn't possible."

I borrowed the scrolls that Apollos had left with Dion. Nerea could not read well, but she picked out the words of some of the hymns we had sung, and I remembered them well enough by now to help her. There was one thing, however, that I was certain she would not be able to understand. I had told her of the death of the young Jew who had been God's son; that his body had been killed, but not how it had been done. Although she was so much better, was her mind strong enough yet even to think of death by crucifixion? I was afraid that might turn her away violently from my faith and I did not know if I was strong enough yet to bear it if she made things hard for me, as she could do so easily.

Dion came home late on the fourth day with his face bleak. "I had to go to a dissertation at the school of Simonides," he said, "and when I finally got to Drusus's workshop they told me that Timas had left this morning, very early."

It was chilly now in the garden courtyard once the sun was down over the roofs. The summer dining-room would not be used again, and already columns of cloud were gathering over the mountains north of the Gulf to bring the heavy autumn rains. I drew the upper folds of my tunic over my arms and shivered. Suddenly the light seemed to have faded from the coming months. With Dion uncertain and Nerea perhaps ill, how would my new faith work day by day when chances to escape for worship to the house of Titus were few, and there was no teaching brought joyfully home from Timas whenever Dion could meet him at the tilemaker's workshop?

"Timas said that we must remember that we aren't alone," I said. "He's been here these last months away from Paulus and all the other people he knew and loved long before he met us. It didn't change him."

"I know, but being unhappy makes me selfish. And, Timandra—you know what he was like. Of course I respected Apollos, but Timas was so like me, as I wish I was."

"Even to the dirt under the fingernails?"

He laughed. "Perhaps even that. Timas said that nothing in our lives happens by accident or can't be used by God. Early lessons in anything seem dull and don't make much sense. I suppose I am being taught something by losing Timas. I don't see what, but perhaps that's because I don't want to look."

I thought he was going to hug me, but then Hegiso waddled through from the atrium and I heard Nerea calling, and the understanding between us was there but we had no way to express it.

That night it rained. The thunder woke Pyrrha and made her restless; she could not understand that it was cooler now at night and that she must sleep under a blanket. All her short life so far she had worn only the wrappings that were there to keep her clean. Now she cried and pushed the covers away with her soft fat arms, or came up from beneath them breathless and crimson. I picked her up at last and lay with her curled in the crook of my elbow listening to the rain on the roof and smelling the wet stone and soaked leaves from the garden.

It was only at times like this that it seemed possible to learn how to pray, as if I was talking slowly, with hesitations, to someone very close to me in the darkness, trying to put into words so much that puzzled and troubled me, things I could not understand or ways where I needed help. It did not seem difficult to talk like this, and at the good times to be full of joy and the thanksgiving that still ran like a deep stream at the roots of my life. What was hard was learning to listen, and to be certain of what I heard and where it came from. The evil and wickedness that were all about us in Corinth so that they had become part of the fibre of our minds could come between me and the true voice of the Master's spirit, which was the clear spring inside that Timas had spoken of.

Pyrrha went to sleep as the thunder faded away south over the mountains of the Peloponnese, and the rain slackened. She would wake if I moved her, so I eased my numb right arm into a more comfortable position and settled to sleep myself. Someone splashed by quietly outside in the courtyard and the faint glow of a lamp moved across the wall. Probably Rufus was going to make sure that the shutters were all secure and none of the gutters was blocked.

Even as sleep took me I prayed for the woman whose child lay so peacefully in my arms.

The ten days passed and Nerea's sickness continued. We could not doubt now that she was pregnant again.

"Were you as sick as this last time?" I asked one morning when she huddled exhausted under the covers in a room that seemed dark and chilly, with an irritable wind rattling the small panes of glass in the high window.

"Yes, I suppose I was, but I seemed to get over it faster. I was hungry by midmorning."

That had been worrying me, already her face was thinner. The time had come when Urbinus must be told. The moment came that evening when he returned home from the baths rather earlier than usual. Nerea was dressed but she had remained in her room on a couch near a small charcoal brazier. Although midwinter was still nearly two months away already she seemed never to be warm; she loved to see and play with Pyrrha who had reached the most delightful age, cheerful, easy, but still immobile in her cot. It was some days since she had picked up her sewing or looked at one of the scrolls with me.

Urbinus came into the room looking large and very handsome, with his toga perfectly arranged, smelling of bath oil. Nerea reached out her hand to him but did not attempt to get up.

Urbinus kissed her very kindly as he always did. "Are you not well? I'm sorry, I've been busy, I hadn't noticed."

I wondered if I should leave them alone together, but a look from Nerea told me to stay. I suddenly realized that this was going to be one of the rare times when she had decided on something that she wanted, and then I had never known her not to get her way.

"No, I'm not too well, but it's not that I'm ill exactly, more interesting than that. Perhaps late next spring, Urbinus, you will have a son. It's rather unexpected, but will that please you?"

Urbinus's face blazed for a moment with joy and he took both her hands; then the light faded and he was full of concern.

"But you're not strong! How long have you known? You should have told me at once."

Nerea laughed. "But I'm not long past two months now, my dear husband. I was hardly sure till a day ago myself, except for the sickness."

"The physician must come to you tomorrow. There is much he can do to make the next few months easier for you. Last time we took too much for granted, and, besides, Hegiso was younger and you had Prisca with you."

Nerea showed me with a smile that I should not feel that he was doubting my care of her. "Yes, of course, and that was something I wanted to speak to you about. I would be so glad, for a month or so, till the early sickness is past, to be near an older woman. Now that the summer's over, with you so much away, the house is very quiet and it could well do without what care I'm able to give it. I thought you might allow me to stay for a while with Chloe."

A stab of joy went through me. This was right and it would help us all so much, if it were possible and Urbinus would permit it. I prayed then urgently and silently.

Urbinus looked doubtful. "Haven't we any near relation who might come to you, and care for you for a while? It would look strange that in our position my wife must go to strangers because she has no company at home."

Nerea gave her most charming laugh. "I know most of your fellow councillors are fathers. They can tell you about the waywardness of pregnant women! Be thankful that I don't yet crave for strawberries at midwinter. May I go just for a while, Urbinus, to be with a cheerful friend and get good advice, so that I can grow strong again and give you a strong son in return?"

I did not think there would be much argument after that and I was right. A message was sent to Chloe and she came herself the next day and seemed delighted at the idea of the visit. I was to go with my mistress, and Pyrrha and her wet-nurse; the men of the household would be looked after by Hegiso and the other women under the guidance of Rufus.

At first I had not remembered Dion. He had been very quiet since Timas went and I had not seen very much of him; there seemed to be some battle going on inside him that he needed to fight alone. The last six months had changed him in so many ways. Something of the glow had gone, he was a young man now, a full citizen, not just a charming boy, yet I did not think Olympias would have disapproved of the changes, the greater seriousness and the understanding. He went dutifully to the classes in rhetoric at the school of Simonides nearly every day, but not with any very great enthusiasm. He seemed to be waiting, as I had seen the shipmasters of Samos waiting through the winter when the seaways were closed and the business of fitting out their galleys for the coming spring did not fully occupy their minds.

A few months ago Dion would have said, "What about me?" at the prospect of a lonely month at home. I had watched for his coming home to be the first to tell him, and now he stood in the atrium with his cloak still close around him, a scroll poking out of the folds in the front, and thought before he spoke.

"Yes, I can see it would be best for Nerea," he said. Then he looked at me closely. "What is it, Timandra? You think she should go, don't you?"

"Yes, of course I do, I'm sure the Lord sent the idea. Only, Dion, I don't think your brother realizes that she's far from well. At best I'm afraid she will carry this baby badly, it's too soon and she isn't strong enough."

"But girls are always sick in the first months from what I've heard."

"It's more than that. Still, we must wait and pray, and Chloe will know what to do. Will you come to see us?"

He smiled, slipping off his cloak and giving it to me; there was a two-sided tear down near the hem. "Of course, or who would mend my clothes or see that my nails are clean?"

However, I saw that night that he was watching Nerea closely, and there was something new behind his eyes, a bleakness and a fear that I had never seen in him before, even during the last hours with Olympias.

Nerea was moved to Chloe's villa in a closed litter, to shield her from the bad weather, not the fears that even now that she was ill seemed to have left her. It was as if she was almost happy to be out in the narrow streets of the city after days of being ill in a small room. Once we had turned off the wide paved road to Laechium the going was muddy, and I was glad to arrive to the warm welcome of Chloe and her household. The physician came to see Nerea again after she was rested from her journey and he talked for a long while with Chloe. After three days Nerea was clearly more cheerful, quite content among her circle of new friends, but still inexplicably weak and now often in pain.

On the fourth day Dion came to see us. He laughed with Nerea and played with the baby, and then when the time came for them both to rest Chloe took us aside into her own small, quiet room. It was warm from the hypocaust under the curious, complicated geometric mosaic of the floor; she sat down in a chair of inlaid citron wood and Dion sat opposite her. As I stood in the slave's place, one step out of the circle, she pointed to a stool.

"Sit down, Timandra. In my house we are brothers and sisters, and that's how I think of you, not as my friend's slave. Besides, I can see you're tired. Nerea slept badly last night, didn't she?"

"Yes, her back was aching. I got up and rubbed it and then she seemed easier."

Chloe spoke to both of us. "You know, don't you, that she's ill? I don't think she will be able to carry this baby, and the physician is afraid of the same thing. Urbinus will have to be told. He will be disappointed, won't he?"

"Yes," said Dion. "He wants a son, but not necessarily yet, not if it would bring danger to Nerea. Do you want me to tell him?"

"Please. He was here two days ago, but I would be glad to see him again before too long, and I daren't leave Nerea at the moment."

"Shouldn't we pray with Nerea, that the Lord will make her strong? Metella was telling me that he healed a woman who had had a haemorrhage for years once. Surely he could strengthen Nerea so that she could have her baby?"

"If it is his will, and he can use what faith we have, of

course he can do it. Don't you think I've been praying almost every hour during these last days for that same thing? And I've asked for prayer from the brothers in the city. But the Lord has not spoken to me clearly about what we should do. Nerea is on the edge of belief herself, she is curious and impressed, but it is difficult often for someone who is sympathetic to take the step forward that makes new beliefs apply to herself."

Dion said, "I know, how I know that." He bowed his head.

"But the Lord chooses the time, doesn't he?" I asked.

"If our blindness doesn't hide it from us."

"What do you think will happen?" I asked.

Metella came quickly into the room. "My lady, I think you should come."

"What is it?" Chloe stood up quickly.

"The Lady Nerea woke a few minutes ago. When I was bathing her face she moved over in the bed and there was a dark stain. I think she's losing blood."

"Did she notice?"

"No, I don't think so. She didn't say anything."

"Dion—" Chloe turned back in the doorway. "Fetch Urbinus and the physician at once. I think things are happening even more quickly than I had feared."

"But if she loses the baby so soon, at three months, that isn't dangerous, is it?" I asked urgently as I followed her into the atrium.

"No, not usually, but I'm uneasy. There is something for which we haven't much time, but I don't know what it is."

Dion had walked to the villa through the fresh sunshine of early winter, but now Metella ran to the stables to call for a horse for him, for he might have to search the city for his brother.

"Timandra, I don't want to go," he said, quickly tying his cloak. "I'm frightened, and I'd rather be here where I know what's happening than away by myself. But I've got to go."

"Go with God, He will be with you and with us," I said. Then I ran to Nerea's room.

Chloe was sitting on the bed looking down at my mistress. Nerea was curled on her side like a small child, but one hand trailed on the covers, and the nails were stained with blood. I saw that she was crying very quietly. So she knew.

"My dear, better now than later. You know it was too soon for you," said Chloe, smoothing back her hair.

"It's the waste of it. My baby's very real to me already, Chloe, even after three months, little Urbinus the younger." Her voice ended in a little gasp and she doubled up as if a cramp had seized her.

Chloe stood up quickly. "Wait here, Timandra, while I fetch what we shall need."

I went over to the bed, suddenly frightened. I had been with my mother twice when neighbours' babies were born, but this was going to be different, with no child at the end of it to put in the arms of a tired, proud woman. Nerea reached for my hands and gripped them, closing her eyes. When the pain eased she managed a small smile but she did not let go. From then on, through all the hours of the night, I was not frightened again, only absorbed with what my fingers and brain and spirit could do for this girl so very little older than me. Nerea was like a young tree being cruelly battered down by the winter gale of life.

Chloe came back, and with her order and activity. She had taken off her overtunic and tied on a large apron, and brought one for me. Two of her women brought in a bowl of warm water and a pile of clean linen. Between us we examined Nerea, who was still bleeding though not much; but it did not cease during the next three hours while the pains came and went but would not settle to the regular pattern that would mean that the business would soon be over and Nerea could rest. We made her as clean and comfortable as we could and then waited for Urbinus.

It was after dark when I heard horses in the courtyard. Nerea had been dozing but roused then, and as Metella brought Urbinus, in his riding cloak, into the room she began to cry.

Although I knew there was no passion between them, he was very tender with her, as he dried her eyes and kissed her hair.

"My dear, it was too soon, and it's better this way," he said, and some of the distress went from Nerea's face. I could see that she must have been expecting angry questions about what she had eaten or what she should not have done. It was clear that Dion had explained what Chloe had told us both.

He came to the doorway, too, and stood there, hesitant about coming in. I went out to him and we stood close together in the dimly lit atrium, talking quietly. He was trembling with more than the cold of the night ride.

"What is it?" I asked. "What are you frightened about?"

"I don't know. Yes I do, though, death. A death like that, very young and not prepared. How can that be part of God's will? Is he asleep?"

"Chloe said once that there were times when the powers of evil are too strong for us. It's as if we are too young in the spirit to be able to deal with them, and then things go wrong."

"But Nerea may die without believing, Timandra. I might die. I could have been thrown from my horse tonight, he stumbled once because I was careless. Then I wondered if it was all worth it. If the Way was right, because it can be so difficult."

He began to cry, not easily, trying to be quiet. I put my arms round him, and he put his head down on my shoulder and shivered so that I held him as tightly as I could. "But who said Nerea would die?" I whispered. "She's only losing her baby early, most women do that at some time. Didn't you know?"

I wanted to go back to Nerea, but she had her husband and Chloe, and Dion seemed to be lost in a darkness that had nothing to do with the night. I felt helpless to do or say anything that could reach him as we stood there, I could not even pray in any words, only a dumb and urgent love for Dion and a fumbling towards the Lord. I suppose I felt like a child whose mother must hurt him to heal him, and who is trying through it still to believe in her love.

Love was the only answer, His love for Dion and Nerea, greater than any I could feel for them.

"Dion," I said. "When you're afraid of death you're afraid of the dark. As if you were sitting in a lighted room with your eyes shut. Do you feel my arms? The Lord's arms are round you, and all of us, even closer than that. It's only that we get numb with all we do and say out of our own selfishness, and we don't feel him."

He loosed himself from me and stood back. "Go to her now and let me be on my own," he said, and went quickly into the darkness.

The physician came then, and there was no more time to remember him. An hour later there was a crisis and convulsions that we could not stop. By midnight it was over and Nerea lay as she had when I first saw her on the night that Pyrrha was born, flat and still in her bed, waxen-faced and drained of life. Urbinus had been pacing the atrium for hours, but no one could tell if Nerea still had the strength to come through this long night. If she could sleep now and live till dawn there would be hope.

Chloe had sent her other women to bed, even Metella, for there was tomorrow to think for as well as tonight, and nothing more to be done for Nerea that the two of us could not do between us. There was another couch in the room and for a while Chloe lay on that while I sat beside the bed. I was almost past weariness, sitting slumped with my weight on my elbows on the bed, very near Nerea to catch any change in her breath. She seemed to be asleep but I thought that the rhythm of her shallow breathing was too quick.

For a moment my eyes almost closed. Then I thought that the faint sound coming from Nerea changed and when I looked her eyes were open, gazing thoughtfully at me. She was conscious and calm. Her eyes moved over to Chloe but she was in a doze and I could see that Nerea did not want her to be woken.

Her fingers moved on the cover and I took them between my own, they were dry and hot. "There was something I wanted to know," she whispered, a tiny thread of sound that I bent low to hear. "Your young God, Timandra. He was a suffering and a dying God, wasn't he? I've been lying here thinking about him, for the last hour, and I understand now. Women would, ones who've had children. They know about life coming through suffering, they do it themselves."

She was quiet for a few moments, her eyes closed, but my heart was pounding inside me. There was thankfulness and love and urgent prayer that Dion would come now, quickly, from wherever he was alone with God, for what Nerea was saying was for him, too. Then I understood the feeling of urgency that Chloe had spoken of only the afternoon before. It was a feeling of a test that was coming and that must be passed at a cost that would not be only my own.

Nerea opened her eyes again, and made sure I was listening. "He died, but death didn't hold him and he came back, didn't he? Like they do in the legends, but this was real, twenty years ago, when my mother was my age. And she never knew. How did he die, Timandra?"

It felt like a blow over the heart. This was what had been coming, but even in a moment of horror I knew I must speak, there could only be truth here and kindness would be cruel. "Nerea dear, the governor of Judea thought his sort of love was dangerous, that it could hurt the State—I suppose it would change it. He had the Master arrested, and there was a sort of trial, and then he was crucified with two criminals."

Her eyes and mouth opened in a soundless gasp and a trace of colour flooded under the transparent skin. "Oh no," I thought, "I've killed her, it was wrong after all." There was a movement behind me, the door curtain dropping. Dion was standing there and his coming had woken Chloe, who had sat up to watch us.

Then Nerea spoke again. "But of course, it would have to be like that. I suppose something in me knew and that was why I was so frightened. Now I've known pain I can understand. He did that for me, didn't he, as I suffered pain for Pyrrha?"

Dion came to the end of the bed; his eyes were blazing in the light of the small lamp. "He suffered like that because he loved you, and because that pain could give you more than mortal life, Nerea. It could bring you back to his Father, beyond death."

"But of course!" She closed her eyes again and her head moved sideways on the pillow. Then she said two more words, first "Pyrrha", and then "Master", before her head moved again and her fingers loosened from mine.

"Go with God," I whispered.

12 · RUFUS

Dion looked like a prisoner on trial, but a very quiet and self-possessed prisoner. Nerea had been dead three days and buried that morning, and now those members of the family whom we saw very seldom, uncles and cousins, were all here to make the usual offerings and say the usual words. All the couches had been pulled out in the dining-room, with Urbinus, Secundus and the oldest uncle in the middle, and Dion as the youngest present at the end of the half-circle.

Urbinus's grief had been genuine. He had cried like a child when I brought him the news of his wife's death, and left to Rufus the arrangements for bringing her body home. I would never forget riding back in a litter in the rain with Pyrrha in my arms. Now grief was overlaid by anger, for Dion had not followed Nerea's body to the family tomb.

He had warned Urbinus, but I do not think the magistrate had begun to believe him or to understand what Dion was talking about. Now, as I moved with Rufus between the tables, I heard him make his defence.

His voice was quiet and unemotional, it was a matter of honesty and of fact as far as he was concerned. "But I did tell you, Urbinus. I know that the ceremonies today were not as Nerea would have wanted them. When she died she was a follower of the Way, as I am. We worship a true God, not painted shadows with temples on the acropolis, or our worthy ancestors in the family shrine. Them we can respect without burning incense."

"You'll be refusing to worship the genius of Augustus next!" said Secundus, raising a flushed face from his winecup for the first time that evening.

"Certainly, or the new Emperor Nero, who is no older than I am!"

Secundus banged his winecup down on the table and the cousins gasped. Then Urbinus shouted—the first time I had ever heard him do so—for what Dion had said could be very dangerous. Old Claudius had died not a month before, and no one knew yet what differences the change from a wise but weary man to a young prince of the headstrong house of the Caesars would bring.

"Be silent. Blasphemy is one thing but treason is something very different. Don't you understand that you risk the safety of the whole family when you speak like that, even inside our own home? Because the Emperor Nero is young and seems mild enough, don't imagine his spies are deaf or that my position would be able to protect you."

"Dion, you have shamed us," said the oldest uncle, a mild man with a long thin neck. "Tomorrow the whole city will know that you did not follow the funeral. Even if you had quarrelled with Nerea, which is nothing strange in any family, could you not show her respect at least in public?"

Dion was sitting up with his hands clasped very tightly on his knees. He looked over at the old man but did not seem to see him. "I loved my sister, as who would not who knew her, more than you who cannot have seen her twice in your life. I grieve for Nerea and I shall mourn her in my own way."

"With the fantastic rituals of the latest mystery that you and your intellectual friends have picked up in the market-place!" sneered Secundus.

The corners of Dion's mouth twitched, and I moved quickly so that he would not catch my eyes. Even at such a moment the thought of Chloe and Titus and the other brethren being called intellectual friends was funny.

"It isn't wise to underestimate what you don't understand," said Dion.

"Don't speak to us now of wisdom," said Urbinus, cold and quiet. "You seem to have shown a singular lack of it. Did I hear you correctly just now, or did you say that my wife was also a follower of this Way you are so full of?"

"Yes, she had only newly come to it, but she died with the name of our God on her lips."

Urbinus's face twisted in pain. It was hard for him to bear that he had not been there and we had, and that a second time words had been spoken, not to him, that he could not understand.

"So what it comes to is that you are setting yourself up against the whole family as its sole member who understands this new truth of yours?"

"Yes, now that Grandmother is dead."

Urbinus brushed the memory of Olympias aside. "If it means more to you than we do, why should we hold you back from where your true interests and loyalties lie?"

Dion stood up slowly and looked at his brother. "You are right to remind me that there are bonds stronger than blood or affection and family custom, but I never thought you would say it like that or on a day like today."

He bowed slightly, turned, and walked quickly out of the room.

Under the babble of voices I was thinking "He'll go before I can speak to him!" But I could not leave the dining-room for some time; there was a hubbub of loud conversation and voices calling for wine, but Urbinus sat tight-lipped and silent. I was certain that only anger had made him speak as he had, and that when he had time to think he would never actually drive Dion from the house.

It was an hour before the guests left, and when the other slaves came in to clear the tables Rufus whispered to me, "Try the summer terrace."

I went through the darkened atrium to the garden court-yard. As I had expected Dion's room was unlit, but Rufus's guess had been right. There was a dark shape in the corner of the terrace that stood out against the pale starlight of the cold still night. Dion was huddled in a heavy cloak, sitting very still.

"I knew you would come when you could," he said, not turning round but knowing my step. From his voice he had been crying.

"Your brother didn't mean what he said." It would be easy to comfort a hurt boy, but Dion was no longer that.

"No, I know he didn't, but—you see—I did. When I leave the school of Simonides as I shall do soon, and abandon the public life Urbinus has planned for me, I know he will still be willing to feed and clothe me, for a while at least. I shall let him till I see clearly what the Lord means me to do, but I don't think that will take very long, and it will be more impor-tant than anything the family could ever have been to me."

He laughed in the dark, calm and certain again now, not yet seeing the road but knowing that it would be there. "Strange that if I had spent the family money like water and made offerings to Aphrodite with every priestess at her temple he would think that much more normal than what I shall probably do."

"What happens first?"

"I shall ask Titus to baptize me. With you the blessing came before the water, for me it seems to be the other way round. I know that only after it will I be strong enough to stand alone— as I shall need to."

"When you go I shall be alone, and I've never been baptized," I said, cold with more than the night air.

"Perhaps we can receive it together," he said. "It should be easier now to leave the house when you need to."

Then the reason for that overwhelmed us both again, and I cried as I had not cried since Nerea's death, and it was Dion who comforted me.

But he had been right about my new freedom, as I very soon discovered. Urbinus seemed to have withdrawn within himself, absorbed by the responsibilities of office and seldom at home. Hegiso rocked all day by the kitchen fire and the slaves came to Rufus for their orders, or after him to me. Two days later it was easy to leave Pyrrha with the wet-nurse and slip away while it was still dark to meet the brethren at the small bath-house Titus had built in the corner of his garden. We received there what the Lord has for all who come to him through the waters that are the symbol of death to the old life.

We were home again before the household was properly awake. When I had seen that all was well and the kitchen work was begun Dion beckoned to me from the doorway of his room. There was a small bundle already strapped on the bed, and everything else seemed curiously tidy, neat and empty, without life now that the former owner would not need it again.

"I'm going now, Timandra," he said, and he was as glad and excited as a child waiting for a holiday. "I shan't leave the city, but I don't want my brother to find me—not for the moment anyway. I've decided to go back to my proper name —Tertius. I expect Urbinus has forgotten I was ever given it, but Dion only seems to fit in with the old life. Anyway, there are lots of Tertiuses about, and one more in the Tilemakers' Street won't be noticed. If you need me you'll know where to find me."

"But what are you going to do?"

"Work and wait and pray. One book has been rolled up

and put away on the shelf; I must wait till the next is put into my hands, it isn't for me to choose. Meanwhile I need to learn to be useful and to make my own living."

I looked at the small bundle, the scrolls, spare sandals, his older tunics and a cloak. "You've forgotten your toga."

"I'm the citizen of a different kingdom now!" He bent, laughing, to kiss me goodbye. "Come to the house of Titus when you can."

And I did, during the winter and the early spring that followed it. It was not too difficult even when Pyrrha was old enough to crawl and spatter porridge on the floor, and the wet-nurse had gone. For those months, in the house that would have been empty indeed without the baby, now Olympias and Nerea and Dion had all gone, I lived a strange life.

From time to time I saw Tertius, as he was now, sometimes across the market-place—a quiet young potter's apprentice in a patched tunic—usually at the meetings of the brethren. Even there I did not always find peace and in a way my new friends seemed more real for that. I knew that I did not see the Way very clearly yet, and it was a comfort that others could make mistakes and recover from them and still love each other. There was news from Ephesus on the first boat west at the beginning of spring, from Timas and Apollos and many others that I did not know, and then another letter from Apollos telling us that he would be in Corinth again by midsummer.

Back in the house I knew I was not a young girl any more. Already I was almost the age that Nerea had been when she died. And I did not feel young; I was the housekeeper of Urbinus Torquartus, the city magistrate, and I was not unhappy. I was waiting, too, for life and faith had taught me now what to expect and how to value present contentment or distress.

Yet, when the day came that has directed the whole course of my life since then, I was not ready. With the warmer days the whole house had seemed to wake and flourish again. There was blossom on the fruit trees and Pyrrha could crawl on a blanket on the warm paving stones of the courtyard. There had been more coming and going than usual for several days, some small dinner parties, and the grim set to Urbinus's face that had been there since Dion had left relaxed to an expression that could only be called self-satisfied. He had never mentioned his brother's name or asked anyone in the house if they had news of him after the first day when he came home late to find him gone. Tertius knew that he had made discreet inquiries about the city, but what his agents had found out and what he thought about it he kept to himself.

On this one day Urbinus came home at midday. He went through into the garden for his noon meal, and then sent Rufus to fetch me. I was a little puzzled by the summons, for he usually gave me whatever orders were necessary before he left in the morning, but I was not expecting anything very surprising; it was most likely to be an inopportune tear in his toga.

Rufus was standing behind his master's chair. I can still remember so clearly how they both looked, and the white rose just out and climbing along the roof of the arcade behind them. Urbinus had been eating cold chicken, and the half-gnawed leg was lying on a silver plate with some olive stones and broken bread.

Urbinus said, "Timandra, you after Rufus should be the first person in the household to hear, before the rumour is all over the market-place. I am going to marry again—the only daughter of old Appius Claudius, Claudia Drusilla."

I murmured what he would expect to hear. My master was right to look pleased with himself, for the lady was very well-born and an heiress, as far as I could remember, living in the care of an uncle. How old she was and what sort of a mistress she would make I could find out from the kitchen girls, who seemed to know more of what went on in the city than I did, although I walked in it more often.

But there would be many changes, for any second wife needs to feel she is mistress of her own household. The quiet days of winter would be gone for ever, I knew at once, and it would remain to be seen what sort of mother she was willing to be to Pyrrha.

However, it seemed that Urbinus had not finished. He was looking at me very kindly, in the way that he had on that first day in Corvus's stable.

"Sit down," he said, pointing to a stool near his chair. "I must talk to you about the changes this will make in the household and in your life."

That was kind, I thought, as I sat down shyly. Yet I did not listen too closely to the details of what Urbinus was saying, what slaves Domina Drusilla would bring with her; it was as if I could already feel in my mind towards something else he was trying to say.

"So you see, Timandra," he finished, "as my second wife will bring her own attendants with her, even her own overseer, she will not need another maid. And perhaps the time has come to make a larger provision for my daughter. Naturally we shall discuss that after the marriage."

No, oh no, he's going to sell me! I thought. After his wife died in my arms. Perhaps that was why, because Nerea valued me. Then I saw for the first time that Rufus was looking at me with a strange intensity.

I felt as if all the blood had run to my face and then out of it, leaving me cold and stiff, but Urbinus seemed to have noticed nothing. "Now this gives me the opportunity to fulfil what was my father's intention when he died," he went on. "Rufus, as you know, was the son of the former overseer of the Chenchraea farm. Although he has served me faithfully here in the house, I believe the life of the country is more to his taste and now I can spare him for the first time. However, he also has a wish to be granted, to which I have been glad to agree. When Rufus leaves this house you will go with him as his wife."

There were no words, no thoughts. I did not move except to put my hands up quickly to cover my face. Of course, confusion and embarrassment were suitable in any young woman on such an occasion; what choice had Nerea or Drusilla been given in their marriage arrangements with Urbinus? One did what one was told, somehow, somehow. There was a short silence, and the kind, official voice went on with good wishes for my happiness, and protestations that as soon as it was possible he would free me. Meanwhile, as he did not say, I was a slave and my body was not my own to give or withhold.

In the first stunned moments, when my heart thundered and I was sick and trapped and humbled, and I wanted to die, one thought came through to me urgently, as if it was being spoken inside my head. It was the knowledge that Rufus was standing there watching me, a freedman not able to go to the girl he has chosen and take her if she is willing. If this must be, then what he would see on my face during the next moments would colour both our lives as long as we were together. Marriage I had feared, and a man even closer than a master to own me, and if that must be, not the man of my choice. Timas, I thought. How narrow this Way is for us, and there is not room for two to walk side by side. But Rufus was a good man, and kind, and it was not his twisted face I minded, and he must never think that might have been so.

Urbinus was waiting for me to speak. I took my hands from my face, slowly, clasping them very tight together, and stood up. "I have not thought of marriage since I have been in this house," I said in a small, flat voice.

"No, perhaps not, how could you? But you have cared

devotedly for my daughter, it is right that you should have the chance of children of your own."

I almost cursed my own unborn children. Then I looked up at Rufus for the first time, and carefully twisted up the corners of my mouth into what I hoped he would take for a smile. He was red with nervousness, standing very stiffly; at my look he let out a deep breath—as if he had been holding it for a long time.

Still looking at Rufus I said, "Perhaps when we leave your house after your marriage we could take Pyrrha with us for the summer. It's hot in the city and the country air would do her good; and perhaps Domina Drusilla would be glad not to take up the duties of a wife and a mother at the same time."

"Now that is an excellent idea," said Urbinus, getting up. Rufus came round to stand beside me, and put an arm lightly round my shoulder. I could feel his heart pounding under his tunic, as mine was, and I remembered the morning of my conversion and how I had heard his heart beat then when he had been gentle with me. Perhaps I should have guessed all those months ago that this might be in his mind.

Urbinus left us together. I could not look Rufus in the face yet, but I reached across and touched his hand where it rested on my shoulder.

"I can see it's difficult for a girl," he said over my head to the white rose bush. "To be told and given no choice. Will you miss the city, Timandra? Could you be content on a farm?" And with me, I knew he meant and could not ask in case I answered no and he was lost.

"Yes," I said, thinking fast as I spoke. "My grandfather in Samos had a farm, I went there as a child." Then I laughed as I had not known I still could. "Do you know, I still have a stone from the beach below his farm? It's the only thing I saved from the galley."

He laughed too, but more with relief, and gave my shoulder a quick squeeze. I turned to face him then.

"But Rufus, will you let me, when I can be spared, come into the city to worship with the others? You know I belong to the Way, married or not or free or not can't change that."

"No, I understand. Not what it means to you, but I know it does mean something . . . something you need. Don't be frightened about that, or . . . about anything."

I thought after Rufus had gone, when I was clearing away the chicken bones and the broken bread, without the Way, my master could have beaten me senseless and I would not have married Rufus. Even now I went hot to think how it would be, night and morning, waking and eating and sharing a life with a man you did not love. It was the lot of most women, but my last months with my father had moved me a little away from it. Strange that for months now I had not thought of my father, and yet soon I would live where he was buried, so I could tend his grave. That would have pleased him and the thought of it calmed me.

I was glad that there was a meeting on the next day. When I told Chloe and Metella they did not seem surprised. Chloe kissed me very kindly.

"You're unhappy now, child, but if this is the Lord's will he will bring you joy and contentment through it, and you will have a good man, which is much better than excitement." Then holding me close for a moment, "Don't forget, he will be even more frightened than you are!"

Tertius had not been at the meeting when I arrived, and that puzzled me, and I was distressed that I might have to go without seeing him and he might hear all my news from someone else.

When some of the brethren had already left and the morning was well on there was a sudden joyful disturbance in the door way and he came in followed by the tall, thin shape of Apollos, still in the wide hat and dusty cloak of a traveller.

"Look, he came today after all, but by the road from Athens, not to Chenchraea. I got the news in time and met him at Isthmea." Tertius was jubilant. "There are letters from Paulus and Jerusalem and messages from Timas."

I could not tell him now, when his mind was full of news of his friend. While the others pressed forward with joyful greetings I went towards the door. It was time I was home anyway, if I was away much longer then I should be missed and there would be questions asked.

Tertius caught me up in the courtyard. I should have known that he knew me too well not to see that something had happened.

"My brother's marrying again, isn't he?" he said. "Titus told me. I'm glad, he shouldn't live in that great house alone, with Secundus away most of the time. I'm sure she'll be kind to you, Timandra, I believe she's quite young."

"I shan't be there to find out." I had not cried up till now, but this time I could not help myself. "Rufus is going to manage the farm and I'm going to marry him."

"And you don't want to?"

"No, but I must."

"Timandra, do you want us, the brothers, to try to buy you, if you're very unhappy? I think we could do it."

Then, when there was a chance of escape, I knew that I did not want it, and that this must be the life the Lord had chosen for me. The road ahead was still dark, but it was my road.

I shook my head. "No, I'm not willing, but I think it will be all right."

"Now that you're not going to be in the city, that makes it easier to tell you that I'm going away too. Apollos told me. Paulus has sent for me to come to him at Ephesus. Timas will be travelling during the summer and he wants another secretary; Timas suggested me. I think it's what I was waiting for."

We had reached the doorway into the narrow street behind the basilica. I had gone out of it so many times before in the last six months, but this time I knew that the road that led away from it would be different. This was another parting like the parting from Timas of the summer before. We would meet again, but not as the same two who stood here now. I wanted to say all this to Tertius, but there was something more important.

"Go with God," I said, loosing his hand, and walking straight, without turning back, towards the Laechium road.

A.D. 67: TIMANDRA AND THE OLIVE TREES

I must have sat for two hours among the olive trees this morning, but I'm glad I did. It has been a long time since I have sat like that, peacefully, to be quiet in my mind with my own thoughts; hardly since before I had small Timas, and now he's nearly four. I suppose a life with two small sons does not leave many empty hours.

What disturbed me was Timas himself, running and calling on a lower terrace. I was stiff when I got up, but luckily even he knows now that he is too big to be carried far, and anyway he was too full of his news to stay still. Father had a visitor and wanted me at once, this minute.

It sounded like business from Urbinus. Strange that I still think of him as my master even though he has been only my patron since he freed me when my first son was born. As I followed Timas down towards the farm buildings I thought how when you have lived in a place for thirteen years you cease to see it, it is just home now—the corner where Nereus my firstborn fell and broke a new tooth, and the byre Rufus built. I passed my little fig tree and the grove where my father is buried; even Pyrrha thinks of the farm as the other half of her home, for she cannot remember as far back as the first summer that she spent here, and how she walked three steps from my arms to Rufus under our vine trellis. In some ways I'm glad that I didn't have a girl myself, for she has always seemed like my eldest child.

My guest was hidden from sight as I crossed the farmyard by the corner of the trellis. I should have thought I would always have known Tertius even from behind and after five years, but I didn't. He seemed broader than last time and the news we have had from Rome has made the first lines on his face.

I hugged him as if he had been my blood brother, till Timas said in his small clear voice, "Why does kissing my mother make that man cry? I like kissing my mother!"

That made Rufus roar with laughter. He picked Timas up and carried him away to play with his brother. I could introduce them both properly later.

We sat looking at each other in silence, smiling. What does one say first after five years? I saw myself suddenly through his eyes.

"Yes, I'm plumper than I was. I suppose it's cooking for the men. You're well." It was a statement rather than a question.

"I've been in Thessalonica for the winter. There are no tilemakers there among the brothers, so I have a new craft now—weaving. It seems to suit me, I was glad to be away from Ephesus, I've spent so long there since Paulus . . . left. We had planned that he was coming back and that I would help him revise his letters, but you know what happened; it was a weary job alone, though I didn't do it all at once. I had everything ready for Lucan when he came last year, all the notes and copies that he wanted for his book. But I'm afraid that when Lucan saw me he stopped being a brother and an author and became a physician. He said I'd been poring over papers too long and I was sent north."

"I've missed it, after the first years. 'Greetings from Tertius, who copied out this letter,' whenever there was news from Ephesus."

"I came down yesterday across the Isthmus and narrowly escaped being taken for forced labour to build the Emperor's canal. He was standing there in a gilded chariot crying 'Faster!' and making his own guard take off their beautiful polished armour and dig with the rest. I don't think that Corinth is the better for being the temporary residence of the divine Nero. Strange to think there were some who had great hopes of him when we were both boys; now he looks fat and evil, and he has brought us so much sorrow." He had stopped smiling.

"I've been into the city no more than I could help since he came at the beginning of the winter, and I shall be glad when Pyrrha is here for her summer visit." Then I laughed. "I hope Secundus was one of the diggers. How he would hate it! He's very important now."

"And Urbinus?"

"He doesn't change, and no, he's never spoken of you. Now I come to think of it I don't think that he's changed at all since that first morning when I saw him at Chenchraea, and we have altered so much. I thought then that he was clean and orderly and he seemed—safe. I suppose he can only seem like that because he doesn't let what happens to other people affect him at all. I wonder when he first stopped letting himself feel things—it was long before Nerea died."

"I don't remember the time when my parents got fever, I was very small, but from something Grandmother said once I I think it must have been then. It must have hurt, being alone and the eldest. But now he has a son."

"Poor Drusilla, they were married eight years first, but she's been good to Pyrrha, and the child loves her little brother."

"And you, Timandra? I think all's well with you?"

"The Lord gave and the Lord took. It was a narrow road

and I wouldn't have missed any part of it. But I still miss Nerea; I've never known another woman so well, even though we were only together seven months. She would have understood how I felt three years ago when I lost my last baby."

"But Rufus has been good to you?"

How could I answer that when it seemed that Rufus still withheld from me the one most perfect thing that I prayed for, that we should follow the Way together? It seemed that on that road I had always been so far ahead that when I called back to him my voice was almost blown away. He would come with me when I asked him, to the meeting house in the city, but he sent the boys to me when they asked questions. I could only wait, as Olympias had waited so long before. My silence had lasted too long, while I thought of all this, but Tertius was wise by now to read such silences.

"Rufus is the strong wall around me that keeps out the storms. Chloe saw he was a good man and she was right. Tertius, how long can you stay with us?" The question had to be asked.

"A few days only, I'm afraid. I'm waiting for news of a ship at Laechium, and for Timas. Yes, dear Timandra, we shall all three be together again, even if only for a day."

"And where does your road lead then?" I asked, smiling, but praying in my heart that it was not towards danger, into the power of a bad Emperor whose beast pits have already taken brothers I have loved.

Tertius has always known what I was thinking, and five years have not changed that. His voice was very gentle when he said, "Timandra, we, too, are going to Rome."

And so I have been lying awake in the dark beside Rufus, who can still sleep because I have not told him yet. I have learned to accept and use so much, that I shall be given what I need now, if I ask for it, the strength to give freely what

A.D. 67: TIMANDRA AND THE OLIVE TREES

cannot withhold, the lesson my husband has taught me. I am remembering the young trees on the hillside in the night wind, with their roots deep in stony soil, and I am glad that I staked the damaged tree straight before I came down to greet my guest.